ROGUE OPS

ROGUE OPS

ROGUE AGENTS OF MAGIC™ BOOK 1

TR CAMERON   MICHAEL ANDERLE   MARTHA CARR

DISRUPTIVE IMAGINATION

LMBPN Publishing
PMB 196, 2540 South Maryland Pkwy
Las Vegas, NV 89109

Version 1.00, September, 2021
ebook ISBN: 978-1-68500-426-2
Print ISBN: 978-1-68500-427-9

THE ROGUE OPS TEAM

Thanks to our beta reader, Larry Omans

Thanks to our JIT Readers:

Wendy L Bonell
Dorothy Lloyd
Diane L. Smith
Dave Hicks
Peter Manis
Zacc Pelter
Jeff Goode

If we've missed anyone, please let us know!

Editor
Skyhunter Editing Team

DEDICATIONS

Dedication: For those who seek wonder around every corner and in each turning page. And, as always, for Dylan.

— *TR Cameron*

To Family, Friends and
Those Who Love
To Read.
May We All Enjoy Grace
To Live The Life We Are
Called.

— *Michael*

CHAPTER ONE

Diana Sheen, formerly Special Agent in Charge and now simply the team leader, grimaced as her gloved hand sank an inch deep into the mud. "Dammit, Rath, whose stupid idea was this, anyway?"

The purple-haired troll, three feet tall and hunched over so his skull didn't hit the wooden surface above them, laughed happily. "Yours. Definitely yours."

She shook her head, the mess that was her hair flopping into her eyes. "It was my idea to take out these losers finally. I'm pretty sure you were the one who suggested that we should go in from underneath."

He cackled again. "Not my fault you're too tall."

She smiled, sighed, and reactivated the comm unit that connected her to the rest of the team. She had turned it off so they wouldn't hear her griping. "Boss and Rambo, still crawling through the mud. Anticipate one minute plus to final position."

Kayleigh, her team's technical expert, replied snarkily, "Move your fat ass, slowpoke."

1

Laughter in various pitches and tones sounded across the comms, and Diana sighed inwardly. *I should have known that girl was trouble from the very beginning and not hired her, regardless of how good she is at what she does.* In truth, she and Kayleigh were more than coworkers and more than the roommates they'd once been. They were friends, which gave the perky blonde wench enough latitude to insult her. *I wish she didn't do it publicly or quite as often.*

Her second-in-command, Cara Benoit, callsign "Croft," replied, "Stark and I are thirty seconds out."

Anik Khan, whose last name was also his callsign, checked in. "Face and Khan, ten seconds."

The deep voice of Hank Stills finished the roll call. "Hercules, in position and ready to go." He sounded bored, probably because Diana had excluded him from the infiltration team. He was their backup, waiting in a delivery truck a couple of streets away from the self-storage facility on the outskirts of New Orleans they were currently infiltrating.

In the many months since their forced departure from their Pittsburgh headquarters—after it became what Kayleigh called a "non-structure" in a giant explosion courtesy of their enemies—and relocation to the vimana in Antarctica, her team had deployed all over the country and to several locations around the world.

Diana's boyfriend and nominal boss Bryant Bates had promised that would be the case when they activated Project Adonis, which formally separated them from federal oversight. On paper, they were supposed to be free agents. In practice, the government still gave them orders with deniability guaranteed by a general lack of paper-work. It worked pretty well for both sides.

She refocused on the task at hand. "Pick up the pace, Rambo." The troll, whose name and callsign both came from Sylvester Stallone movies due to his obsession with the silver screen, ran faster.

He could've shrunk small enough not to need to crouch, but the tech genius had sized his tactical gear for the three-foot form he preferred, claiming it gave him the best blend of agility and strength. He was hers, she was his, and they would be together forever. The magic bond connecting them both activated when she'd rescued him at the start of her federal career.

They'd come a long way since then, fighting monsters that looked like monsters and monsters that looked like humans. *Or run-of-the-mill folks from Oriceran, maybe.* Her team's overriding goal had been to gather as many Rhazdon artifacts as possible. The malevolent magics long ago created by a tyrant from the magical planet were too dangerous to circulate freely.

They'd rounded up quite a lot of them, but there always seemed to be more. Her information indicated that a finite number existed, but somehow, she doubted it. *Either someone else continued creating them after Rhazdon was gone, or the bastard simply lied about how many they produced.* Today's operation would bring them several, though, if their info-mancer's research proved to be accurate.

The others reported being in position before she and Rath made it to the spot she'd chosen. Kayleigh and Deacon had given the place a thorough inspection with drones ahead of the infiltration. They had found this unexpected access route, an excavated area used for drainage because of the high water table. They'd also discovered that the central set of eight garages weren't garages at all but a single large building with a lot of heat signatures inside it.

Ultrasound scans had modeled the interior. They weren't *really* ultrasound, but every time Kayleigh tried to explain how the sonic sensors worked, Diana's mind glazed over, so she'd decided to call it ultrasound.

It was a large room, empty of identifiable furniture or inner walls but filled with crates and boxes of various sizes. Two trucks had pulled in to make deliveries while they had the location under surveillance, but their drones hadn't been able to get low enough to peer inside without risking detection.

We need to figure out how to scale up that cloaking tech Ruby created. Their recent efforts had led them to Ely, Nevada, the so-called Magic City with its magical-owned casinos. While there, Diana had connected with a local techno-mancer, a woman who blended magic and technology to create cool stuff. Kayleigh could do the same to some degree, working with Deacon, but Magic City's defender had a gift for the work.

Her inner voice criticized, "That's not relevant right now." *Shut up, you.* Diana shook her head to clear it. Ahead of her, Rath pressed a flat cylinder onto a section of the wooden surface above them, then backed away from it. She said, "We're ready to go."

Kayleigh replied, "Countdown begins."

Her team all wore glasses or goggles, depending on their preference. They connected to a shared tactical computer the tech managed during big operations. Diana's were mostly filled with a thermal image of the bodies in the room above as she looked upward, plus a clock counting down from ten. The rest of her people had similar displays, customized to their preferences.

Diana's also included a series of green dots that represented the health of each of her subordinates. They would change to yellow in case of serious injury and red to indicate critical damage that required immediate intervention.

Their uniforms contained integrated bio-monitors among a plethora of other useful gadgets and systems. Since their earliest days as a new unit, improving their tech beyond what the government had to offer had been as much a crusade as a priority, and they'd worked hard to ensure they were always on the bleeding edge. *Except for drone cloaking, apparently. Kayleigh, you slacker.*

She grabbed Rath's arm and pulled him to her side because he tended to want to rush into battle ahead of her. She was protective of him, and he was equally protective of her, which occasionally put them at odds. The clock hit zero and the explosive he'd placed detonated, creating an irregular rectangular hole and sending splinters flying out at their enemies. Diana crawled forward and launched herself through the opening.

No surprises awaited her, meaning that the recon Kayleigh and Deacon had performed was once again top-notch. Diana lifted her modified M4 carbine and pressed down on the trigger, firing a three-round burst at the nearest enemy.

Had she been shooting at a human, that would've been sufficient to make it a very bad day for them. However, the seven-foot-tall Kilomea, a giant with a leather tunic and a rough-hewn, square-jawed face, only grunted at the impacts and continued to move forward to engage her, one hand pulling a huge knife tucked through his belt. She snapped, "Possible body armor."

Kayleigh, callsign "Glam," replied, "Acknowledged."

A pair of knives flew past her on either side, tumbling through the air to stab into the Kilomea's shoulders. The creature growled and crossed its arms to yank them out, then threw Rath's weapons at her head. She took one hand off her rifle and waved it, using her telekinesis to redirect the blades toward an empty spot to her left. Then he was too close to shoot, so she dropped the rifle to dangle from its strap and stepped forward to meet him.

Cara waited while the explosive cord did its work, cutting a hole in the roof and dropping the metal piece it had severed into the building. She leapt through the opening, using her magic to land softly on a burst of force. The view in her glasses had prepared her for landing in the middle of a group of enemies, too tightly arranged to engage with her rifle.

Instead, she drew the pair of pistols from drop holsters on each thigh and lifted them, shooting directly to her right and left with arms outstretched, three rounds center mass, like she'd learned in the military and as official guidelines required. Two humanoid forms fell away, her mind categorizing one as a wizard and the other as some kind of elf. Another of the six—now four, as the pair she'd shot dropped out of the picture—surrounding her went down as her partner Tony, the team's most proficient marksman, used his position on the roof to good effect.

Three remained, and they forced her to dive aside as a fireball blasted through the spot she'd occupied and continued through the opening she and Stark had created in the circle. *Nice job of adapting. These folks aren't pushovers.*

She spun up to her feet and shoved her pistols back in their holsters. Anik and Sloan had entered the fray, breaking in through one of the garage doors, and now the bodies were mixed up enough that a stray bullet might be bad. Sure, they all had excellent body armor, but it was always possible that the wrong shot at the wrong angle could wind up doing serious, even fatal damage.

Cara slipped to the side of the nearest foe and rammed a knee up into his groin. The man—this one was a Light Elf, as opposed to the Dark Elves, the Wood Elves, and the Mist Elves—doubled over, as a strike to his junk had the same effect as it would on a pure human. She smashed a punch into his jaw, her stun glove going off with a *snap* and dropping him unconscious to the floor.

She continued that move's momentum into a spin and delivered a backfist to another elf who was sidling into an attack. It caught the woman above her ear, and the stun blast dropped her onto her face. Cara shook her head. "Not quite the A-Team. Maybe the B-team."

Rath laughed. "I love it when a plan comes together."

At that moment, a shimmering emanated from several locations in the warehouse as magical portals opened and enemies flooded through. Diana gave an audible sigh and said, "See, Rambo, this is what happens when you tempt fate."

The troll cackled again. "More bad guys available, more fun knocking them down."

Cara smothered a grin at the troll's optimism and headed for the nearest newcomers, ready for some of the fun he'd promised.

CHAPTER TWO

Diana flinched as the magic deflector set into her vest cracked, expending its protective power by sucking away a blast of shadow magic that had sought her. With the battle transforming into a scrum with the new arrivals, crossfire made guns too risky, so she reached over her shoulder and drew her sword from its back sheath.

Fury was the standard length for a katana, but as a magical artifact weapon with a sentient being inhabiting it, it was far more deadly than an ordinary blade. She'd developed a synergy with the sword, and her senses grew sharper with it in her grip, allowing her to identify and defend against attacks more effectively and find optimal angles for her assaults. Combined with her magical sixth sense about harmful magic targeting her, those abilities made her devastating against humans and magicals alike.

She skipped forward and snapped out a sidekick at the Kilomea's knee, but he gave a deft twist and took the blow on his thigh instead. His fist crashed out at her, but her free hand deflected it out of line so that when it finally grazed her chest, it had lost almost all its power. She grinned at the huge figure. "This is no time to make advances on me. Keep your hands to yourself."

The taunt caused his face to screw up in anger, which switched quickly to pain as she lunged forward and drove Fury's point through his shoulder. With the proper twist and yank, she could've severed the limb but instead drew it out the way it went in, then leapt in the air and smashed the hilt into his nose. The giant creature fell backward with a loud *thump*. Diana gave him a kick in the head to make sure he stayed down and looked around to find her next target.

Rath had already thrown all six of his knives, two at the Kilomea and one each at witches and wizards who had targeted him and his partner. While Diana had proven on any number of occasions that she was completely capable of handling herself without his protection, he was committed to making sure she didn't have to when they were together.

When they'd operated from their Pittsburgh base, circumstances had frequently required them to work apart. Now that his skills had improved to equal that of any agent in her group, thanks to endless training at the vimana with the rest of the team, he'd probably wind up on his own even more often going forward.

For now, in this place, his primary goal was to watch her back whether she wanted him to or not. He reached down to his thigh holsters and drew his batons, flicking them out to full extension with a satisfying *snap*. Each contained an electrified tip fed by a battery on the rear of his belt. When he held them in his gloved hands, induction pads on the palms completed the circuit.

He had Kayleigh and her mentor Emerson to thank for that. The older man was even better than the tech at making weapons and gadgets, which was saying something. He'd continued working with them on the down-low to improve his gear since their relocation.

A Dark Elf was nearby, the very picture of a stereotypical Drow. Black leather armor covered his body, and his head had the expected white hair, pointed ears, and mean snarl. Rath had met many who didn't carry that attitude, including Diana, who was part Drow. So, he figured it was a choice, one he wasn't particularly impressed with. He raced at the man and shouted, "I have a very particular set of skills."

Lately, he'd been on a Liam Neeson movie binge and appreciated the actor's no-nonsense approach to combat situations. The elf sent a blast of fire at him, but the magic deflector in Rath's vest sucked the flames away without letting any escape to damage him. The faceted crystal didn't make a cracking sound, so he knew it was good to deal with at least one more incoming attack. It wasn't guaranteed to fully block the next spell since the Drow's first try partially compromised it. *Which must not have been very powerful to begin with. Loser.*

He reached his target and slapped the batons out at the man's legs, forcing him to backpedal to avoid having his shins broken. Rath continued, "Give up, and that'll be the end of it." *Not a perfect quote, but a little poetic license is appropriate.*

Daggers appeared in the Drow's hands. He slashed both of them down at Rath from the outside in, trying to carve into his chest. The FAM's—Federal Agents of Magic, one of several nicknames they used for themselves—vests were better than the standard versions at defending against knives, but they still weren't perfect. *Besides, no idiot criminal is going to slice up my gear.*

He flicked both batons up in rising crescents to smack into the man's wrists, driving them outward enough that he could dash through the opening he'd created. He leapt into the air and smashed the top of his head into the bottom of his opponent's jaw. The unexpected blow knocked him backward.

Rath saw a few stars from the impact, but fortunately, trolls had pretty thick heads. *Well, at least this troll. Gotta protect the big brain.*

He chuckled at his joke and stabbed out with the batons as soon as he landed. Both of them connected with the Dark Elf's chest, and the electric tips caused him to jitter in place before falling senseless to the floor. His knives clattered beside him. Rath spared a glance to ensure the man was out, then ran for the portal nearest Diana, which continued to discharge enemies at an alarming rate.

Cara stopped in her tracks and shook her head at the sight ahead of her. "Are you guys twins?" *They look more like clones, really.*

The pair of elves standing six feet away nodded in perfect synchronicity. Both wore fancy white leather, somewhere between biker gear and actual armor, and carried paired swords. Their facial structure was the same, the only difference being that one's long white hair held more curl than the other. She said, "That second *Matrix* movie was a long time ago. You should maybe consider finding a new shtick."

They scowled in unison, and the one on the left said, "You'll pay for that."

The one on the right finished, "Bitch."

Cara shook her head. "You should know; I do *not* like that word." She drew her pistols and strode forward, firing two-handed, three rounds at each of the elves. They spun in opposite directions to avoid the bullets, clearly intending to come at her from both sides with their swords. "Oh no, you don't," she growled. She shoved the guns back in their holsters and launched herself into the air on a blast of force magic.

Flight wasn't something she'd ever been good at, but Diana had insisted that everyone practice the things they weren't good at, and now she was capable of managing small, controlled hops. She wouldn't be flying rooftop to rooftop like some of the magicals she'd met, but her skills were adequate to get her out of the way of their swords as they slashed in at the space she'd occupied.

As her feet hit the floor, she blasted darts of flame from her fingers, sending five at each of them. One dropped his sword and waved, creating a slightly translucent magical barrier in front of him that intercepted and dissipated her offensive magic. She muttered, "Okay, you want to get up close and personal? Let's do it, then."

Cara drew her paired daggers, each about the length of her forearm, from the sheaths on her thighs. As always, Angel was in her right hand and Demon in her left. The blades' inhabitants spoke to her as she moved forward, reminding her of the instructions they'd given her in the past about fighting longer weapons. The sentient weapons were *very* concerned with her combat ability and constantly sought to make her better. *Sometimes, though, not at the best moments.*

She let the message, *Not right now, please,* float through her mind and engaged the twins. Her angle of approach to the nearest prevented the more distant one from engaging her without going around his partner. Her opponent was skilled, not randomly slashing, but instead bringing his left blade down in a high arc to force her to commit to blocking it, then stabbing quickly with the other, seeking to pierce her stomach. Metal rang against metal as she intercepted the first easily and the second with a slightly more frantic block.

Cara whipped her left leg up in a crescent kick that smacked into the inside of his elbow and drove his right arm and the sword it held out to the side, then stabbed in with her left dagger, keeping his other weapon at bay with her right. He shifted, stepping out and back with one foot, and her thrust passed in front of his now perpendicular body. He chambered and kicked out at her every bit as quickly as her attack, and she accepted the blow without giving up any ground.

The impact flowed through the vest into her tight

stomach muscles, which she'd braced for the strike. She was surprised at how much it still hurt. The pain wasn't relevant at the moment, only her next move.

She threw herself forward, not wanting to surrender her position inside his blade's reach, and slammed the pommel of her right-hand dagger down at his face while punching into his shoulder with her left fist. Both blows connected. The stun wasn't powerful enough to affect him through his armor, but the metal smashing into his cheekbone was entirely sufficient to shatter it.

He stepped back reflexively with a cry. She pulled her arms in, then snapped them back out, thrusting forward with both blades. They speared through the chest of his leather tunic, and he fell, her weapons sliding easily out of his armor as he tumbled away.

Her instincts, or maybe the daggers, screamed a warning in her head. She dropped and spun backward, sticking out a foot to sweep the legs of the other elf, who had moved in on her blind side while she was fighting the first. He jumped over her leg and slammed his swords down at her with a triumphant look on his face.

Cara released her daggers and called up a staff of force that stretched between her hands, intercepting both weapons a couple of inches away from her head. She rose as he tried to withdraw the blades, keeping the magical rod in contact with them, and pistoned her knee into his solar plexus.

He gasped and coughed, his attention fully devoted to trying to remember how to breathe. She put her foot down, drove her other knee into his groin, then delivered a spinning back kick to his temple as he crumpled. He flew sideways to stretch out on the floor.

She reached out with telekinesis and pulled the daggers back to her hands. A glance toward movement in the corner of her eye made the blood inside her turn to ice at the same moment Diana said, "Shit. They're not only moving the artifacts. They're using them."

CHAPTER THREE

The appearance of tentacled enemies changed the calculus for the battle. Diana snapped, "No restraint," and ran at the nearest. Her senses whispered a warning, and she threw herself to her left in a flip to evade the bolts of shadow magic that attempted to strike her from behind. She cursed and circled another enemy, using them as a barrier to keep the shadow bolts away from her, and found a clear path toward the foe she sought.

He was a tall, red-haired elf with a long scar on one side of his face. The whitened ridge on his skin was less impressive than the shadow tentacles spiraling from his left arm and seeking Rath's nimble form. She growled, "Get away from my partner," and used her free hand to whip out a line of force. It wrapped itself around the tentacles, grabbing them and pulling them from their target. The troll, who'd presumably detected who she was going after and decided to help, dashed in with his batons and swung at the tendrils she'd missed with her snare.

The enemy knocked one of the weapons out of his

hand, and it flew aside with a clatter. Diana let the force line go, pulled the pistol from her right thigh drop holster, and walked steadily toward the elf, pulling the trigger in carefully measured bursts. As soon as she'd drawn, he'd responded with a sneer and a wave of his non-artifact arm to create a shadow shield.

While that might've been effective against normal rounds, she and her team always loaded their pistols with anti-magic bullets, and usually the rifles as well. The first round punched through the barrier and took him in the shoulder. The next struck him mid-chest. She lowered her aim and put one into his hip, and he cried out and fell to the floor in agony. "Tie him up, Rambo."

Rath ran to the fallen elf and managed to get a zip tie around first his ankles, then his flailing hands, immobilizing him. The pain of the wounds was doubtless interfering with his magical control, as tentacles kept trying and failing to materialize from the artifact. *Working as intended.* She'd chosen the hip shot knowing that breaking that bone in particular would be extraordinarily painful. The troll took a longer zip tie and connected the other two, leaving the elf bound in an arc, almost forming a circle because Rath had pulled the bonds so tight.

Diana nodded. "Good work, buddy. On to the next."

Diana's command let her team's full fury loose. Cara sheathed her daggers and jerked up her rifle. She dashed for cover behind a bunch of boxes, then peeked up over the top to sight her enemy.

The nearest foe was a dwarf, conspicuous due to the strange topknot he wore that funneled his hair into a small column before letting it spill out like a weird fountain. A plethora of objects entwined in his beard—*Is that bone?*—added to the effect. He was surrounded by a weaving shield of shadow tentacles, courtesy of the artifact in his left arm. His right hand held an ax, and he was in motion, angling in the direction of where she'd last seen Khan.

Even if the demolitions expert weren't currently sharing her bed on occasion, she would have still felt compelled to defend him from the threat. He didn't have magical abilities unless you counted his explosives proficiency, which was seemingly more than human. She pulled the trigger and held it down, dispatching rounds at the dwarf. He was smart, or lucky, and ducked out of the way at the right moment to avoid the stream of bullets.

Her rifle barrel tracked him as he moved, but the rounds buried themselves in the side of a dilapidated box truck. With a snarl of frustration, she put one hand on the boxes in front of her and vaulted them, bringing her gun in line with where she'd last seen the dwarf. A creaking warned her, and she wrapped herself in a cocoon of force magic an instant before the truck scraped along the floor sideways at high speed.

It slammed into her and hurled her into the air, sending her crashing into another stack of crates a quarter of the way across the warehouse. The upper ones fell on top of her, straining her magical strength as she maintained her shield against them. Cara had never been the most powerful magical, which had led her to prefer technological modes of combat where possible. Under Nylotte's tutelage, she'd been developing her magical pool. It was far better than it had been when she joined Diana's team, but it still wasn't sufficient to handle an entire battle using only arcane powers.

Tony murmured in her ear, "I've got you." A pair of shots rang out from his position on the roof, and a moment later, he said, "Target down. Watch out. The artifact's free." That warning informed the team that the host had died, and the physical legacy of Rhadzon's evil phase would be seeking a replacement. None of them wanted that burden, regardless of the power that came along with it.

They'd had many a late-night conversation in the vimana on that topic over drinks, knowing they were a minute's walk away from the vault that held dozens of the magical items. Despite the mandate to turn them over to the government, Cara estimated Diana had surrendered maybe one in three. When asked why, the team's leader said, "I don't trust them with this much power. We'll keep our own eyes on it."

No one on the team disagreed, at least not in public. She wholeheartedly shared the view and probably would've turned over fewer. Finally, the boxes stopped falling. Cara used telekinesis to push them off her, then rose to her feet. "Stark, vector?"

"At your two o'clock, pair of magicals. Melee weapons."

She nodded and hefted her rifle. Experience had taught her that ranged fire was the single best answer to enemies looking to engage in hand-to-hand combat. "On my way."

Rath retrieved his baton from where the tentacled scumbag had thrown it and frowned at the mangled tip. "You got what you deserved, jerk," he muttered and turned to find a Kilomea bearing down on him with a giant club in its hand. *Correction, giant* spiked *club*, Rath thought as the object swung through the air at him. He leapt backward in a somersault, taking advantage of his three-foot body's natural agility to get him moving.

In midair, though, he started to grow. By the time his feet were back on the floor, some pieces of his gear had fallen away, and others were hanging from his now seven-foot form, which was as heavily muscled as the Kilomea, making them a good match. He dropped his batons and swept forward, grabbing his opponent's hands before he could start a backswing.

Diana had been teaching him the various martial arts she knew, and one of the things he'd learned was a series of effective joint locks to use from any angle. With a deft twist and a lift, he locked out the Kilomea's elbow and used it to propel him into motion. Like any creature with an ounce of sense, his enemy preferred *not* to have his elbow joint shattered by being bent in the wrong direction, so he moved.

Rath reversed his hold suddenly, yanking down and forcing the Kilomea to leap and flip to avoid that same breakage. The move caused him to fly out of Rath's grasp, but that was fine because the club stayed behind. When the Kilomea rose to his feet again, he faced an angry, seven-foot, muscular, purple-haired troll with a spiked club. The troll laughed as he remembered a similar object being used in *Escape from New York* and said, "Call me Snake."

The Kilomea tilted his head as if he didn't understand, and Rath frowned sadly. "Uncivilized. Uncivilized weapon, uncivilized person. Sad." He hurled the club up to the catwalk that followed the building's outer walls, a story and a half above, and ran at the Kilomea. His opponent braced and intercepted the first punch Rath threw his way. A grudging admiration appeared for the other creature, as he hadn't only blocked the blow, he'd caught it.

Then the feeling faded as the giant tried to crush his hand in a typical display of dominance. *Strength isn't always the answer, dumbass.* Rath thrust his left fist in at a punch toward the Kilomea's chest. When his foe's free arm moved in to block, as expected, Rath pulled the attack back then punched down, slamming his fist into the creature's groin.

While he'd lost the connection to the battery on the rear of his belt when he'd changed forms, the techs had specially designed Rath's gloves to hold a single charge when detached from power. The stun blast went off on impact, and the creature folded and fell to the floor, keening in agony. The troll bent and tapped him on the temple with the other glove, sending him into a merciful unconsciousness. "Idiot."

He stood and ran toward Diana, who looked like she was in trouble.

I might be in trouble. Diana had charged one enemy, only to find herself suddenly in the middle of three, each of them with an artifact. She'd thrown herself into the mental connection with Fury, and together they spun, dodged, and sliced, intercepting and severing tentacles that sought to capture her. They achieved only a stalemate because while having the tentacles cut hopefully at least caused her foes pain, the artifacts created more to replace the damaged ones almost instantly.

She lunged a few times, trying for a killing blow to the throat or heart, but the trio operated well as a unit, her target fading back as his pair of allies used the opportunity to attack her. She had options, including grenades on her belt that might work as enough of a distraction to allow her to strike, but the arrival of her partner in his largest form forestalled the need.

Rath slammed into the one on her right, leaving the ones at twelve and nine o'clock momentarily surprised. *Giant troll with purple hair will do that.* Diana took advantage of the moment to slash at the nearest, twisting to angle her blade perfectly to slice into and through the man's arm, just above where the artifact rested near his wrist. The limb fell, and immediately a physical object shaped like a black widow spider emerged from it, grew legs, and scuttled back toward its host.

Diana kicked it, sending it flying. A wave of her free hand summoned a dome of force to cover it when it landed, and she detailed a piece of her mind to the task of maintaining that barrier as she continued to fight. She spun, accepting the grasp of her last foe's tentacles around her waist in trade for the opportunity to slam her elbow into his face. He stumbled back, and she smacked him in the head with the flat of her sword, almost a baseball swing, knocking him stumbling further.

Before he could regain his balance, her shock glove

snapped as it smashed in his nose. He fell, unconscious. Diana looked around to find that Rath's opponent was also down, and most of the enemies who were capable of doing so had fled through their portals, leaving the battlefield to them.

She pushed the hair out of her eyes with a curse. "Damn cowards, running away and taking their artifacts with them. Stark, stay on overwatch. Khan, Face, do a sweep, and clean up the magic items you find. Rambo, give them a hand. Croft, interrogate anyone who's still conscious. You all know the drill."

Cara replied, "Not helping out, boss?"

"I have a thing. I need to get moving. This took longer than expected."

Sloan Woodham, the team's spy, said in a lascivious tone, "And by *thing* you mean Bryant, our big boss. Your boyfriend."

Cara added, "Or perhaps she means Bryant's thing."

Diana sighed. "All of you, shut the hell up and get to work." But she said it with a smile, and she was still grinning as she portaled back to the vimana to get ready for her long-delayed date night with Bryant.

CHAPTER FOUR

Bryant Bates stepped out of the portal in the same spot he always did, a small service hallway that held the single gap in the building's anti-magic defenses. The Senate complex was a maze of hallways and offices, some at ground level, some above, some beneath. His contact had been moved into a newly built, even lower excavation several months before, and Bryant found his way to the staircase that led downward.

He'd tucked a piece of tech Emerson had designed inside the knot of his tie. It would cause the video cameras to see either a fuzzy image of his face or one too blurred to make out. The sophisticated watch on his left wrist connected to it wirelessly to assist in its work. The powerful computer, similar to the ones the agents wore in their tactical gear, also fed the thin, round-framed spectacles perched on his nose. They were a custom version of the agent's glasses because he needed to stand out rather than resemble them for political purposes. *Gotta seem like the boss, not part of the crew.*

He knocked on the door of Finley's office, and a voice from beyond said, "Come." He strode in, and his closest government ally rose from behind his elegant wooden desk to shake his hand. "Bryant, always good to see you. Thanks for stopping by."

He took one of the seats across the polished surface as the man lowered himself back into his own. The senator from Rhode Island's normally crew-cut brown hair was a little long today, but he still held himself with a decidedly military bearing, as fit his background. "So, I hear your team is out on an op today?"

Bryant nodded. "Same old, same old. More artifacts to gather. I'm starting to think the number we received was incorrect, that the bastard created more of them. Or maybe someone followed up on Rhazdon's work somehow."

The senator raised a perfectly trimmed eyebrow. "You have evidence of that?"

He sighed and reclined in his seat, shaking his head. He tapped the metal bracelet on his right wrist on the chair's arm, a habit he'd developed shortly after receiving the illusion detection device. "When do I ever have solid evidence of anything? We operate mainly on innuendo, guided by word on the street. My folks are as much a group of detectives as a team of tactical agents."

Finley nodded. "The magical FBI, yeah, I get it. Listen, people are talking, which is why I wanted you to come in."

Bryant replied, "People?"

His reply was decisive and serious. "People. Who shall not be named, even in this office." Bryant looked around suspiciously. "Yes, it's been checked for listening devices this morning, as always. Don't worry, I believe in my government, but I don't trust the people in it blindly."

He nodded. His watch had also searched for surveillance the moment he'd entered the room, and the overlay in his glasses had reported that they were clear. *Still, I've been accused of paranoia once or twice, and not inappropriately.* "So, I don't get to know what kind of people are talking, but I presume they're either notably placed or the subject under discussion is important."

Finley nodded. "Both. Bluntly, folks are wondering whether your team has too much latitude. That, of course, is cover for what they *really* think, which is that your girlfriend is amassing a little arsenal of magical items. Naturally, she'll use them to overthrow the White House or some such thing."

Well, part of that might not be too far off the mark. While Diana would never take action against the government any more than he would, he was pretty sure not every item and artifact her team recovered found its way into the official record. They'd never discussed it explicitly. Instead, they'd engaged in their little version of don't ask, don't tell to allow him to speak truthfully on the matter if anyone questioned him. Bryant shrugged. "Possible. I can honestly say I know nothing about it."

Finley nodded. "Smart." The two men exchanged smiles. "That doesn't change the fact that important people are asking difficult questions. Eventually, they'll move from talking over drinks to talking in committees, or worse, subpoenaing the principals involved. I don't imagine you or Diana would enjoy that experience much."

"Nor do we have time for it. I appreciate the heads up,

though. I'll make sure I keep an overnight bag packed in case I get summoned. Is that all that's worrying you?"

Finley shook his head. "There's a particular pair of senators that have been speaking more harshly than the rest. Interestingly, they're bipartisan, from the same state."

Bryant laughed. "The one thing our government manages to get both parties to agree to is harassing my team?"

The other man shrugged and gave a soft snort. "Right? Seems like a strange happening, but that's politics for you. Anyway, they're discussing taking specific actions without going through the arduous process of gathering facts."

Bryant frowned. "Like what?"

"Congressional oversight. Probably *public* congressional oversight, given the way they're talking."

"You mean changing the team's mandate? Bring them formally under government control again and let the world know they're there?"

The other man replied, "I could see it going in that direction. Which is why I wanted to make sure to inform you. Because if the team does go visible, any corners they cut, any secrets they kept, might find their way into the light as well."

This will put a damper on my date with Diana. He shook his head and rose, sticking out a hand. "Thanks, Aaron. I appreciate your candor, as always."

It took his ally a moment to get up from his chair, and when their hands met, a hard plastic object pressed into Bryant's palm. He released the other man's grip and held the item in place as he dropped his hand to his side. He'd pocket it later, not wanting to seem too obvious about it in case eyes were watching that neither of them had detected. Finley gave him a serious look, though his tone was light. "Be careful out there, my friend."

He nodded. "Will do. Thanks again, Senator." *For the warning, and for whatever this thing is.*

Bryant climbed behind the wheel of his SUV in the garage under his apartment building. If his team was under investigation or observation, he held little doubt that he was, as well. The notion of people doing surveillance on the vimana made him chuckle inwardly. *If anyone's down there in Antarctica keeping an eye on Diana, I hope they dressed in layers. A lot of layers.*

He drove out of the city and into the suburbs, pulling in at a diner he frequented at least once a week when he was in town, usually more. He found a table along the window-covered outer wall, ordered a big breakfast although it was the dinner hour, and headed for the restroom. Normally he'd use the food-prep time perusing websites on his phone or texting with Diana, but that item was currently locked in a signal-blocking case in the SUV's armrest. It was a highly secure device, but he still didn't want it coming with him where he was going.

It was probable that the government would find his car fairly easily, even though he regularly removed the trackers that inexplicably wound up upon it. He assumed they were from his side since he wasn't very visible to the world's criminal element but treated them all as hostile acts. For what he planned, he didn't need too much time, maybe seven minutes. So, if they got there even after a few of them, his visit to the restroom wouldn't seem outrageously long. He closed the stall door, opened a portal, and crossed the threshold to his secret bolt hole.

Most agents had something like it, a safe place they could retreat to, usually containing survival gear and other necessities. He had multiple locations to stay in and equipment stored in several different places, being a paranoid sort. This one, though, was his most secretive and best hidden. It was a featureless room with poured concrete walls, floor, and ceiling, forming a rectangle about ten feet in one direction and five in the other. The most appealing thing about it was that it had no doors and was concealed entirely in the subbasement of an old building.

One of the smaller walls held a set of shelves with food, water, weapons, and medical supplies, along with eight prepaid phones, still in their packages. None of that interested him at the moment. What he needed was on the other side of the room.

A beat-up table supported a desktop computer with a large monitor. It was running an out-of-date operating system because it had never once connected to the Internet. Kayleigh and Deacon had built it for him, and he'd brought it straight here when they'd finished it. He hit the button to power it up, electricity provided by a secret tap into the building's supply. He slid the flash drive that Finley had passed to him into the appropriate slot and called up the contents.

His concern increased with each new layer inside the folder. One section was marked personnel, and in it, he found the official government files of all the people who worked for ARES, both Diana's team and the units in other cities. He was somewhere between impressed and appalled at the amount of detail they'd gathered.

Diana's file mentioned Rath, and Cara's included a suspicion that she was dating another team member. *Where the hell are they getting that information? Audio surveillance while they're in the field, maybe? I can't imagine they've cracked the base's systems or the encrypted comms. Kayleigh and Deacon would never let that happen.*

The next folder held blueprints. Each of the ARES locations was present, with complete building schematics. He'd reflexively assumed that they wouldn't include the vimana since both it and Diana's presence in it were top secret. Still, it too was rendered in all its two-dimensional line-representation glory.

It didn't include the alterations Diana's team had made, which was the first moment of relief he'd had since clicking on the flash drive. It meant no one had infiltrated to see it, that their efforts to keep official guests away from discovering the changes had been successful. There hadn't been many visits, but there had been some. Still, it was a lot of information that, by all rights, should've been kept more secure than this.

He clicked through the rest: records of salary payments, vehicle identification numbers for the cars allocated to the teams, even credit card statements of the Special Agents in Charge. He smiled when he came across the email repository because the first one he saw was from Emerson, and it was a list of complaints about how he wasn't getting the supplies he needed. Bryant had heard the man say such things in person so many times that it was like an old friend tapping him on the shoulder.

When he finished with his quick survey of the information, he leaned back with a sigh. *Okay, it's not good, but we can deal with it.* Bryant shoved the flash drive in his pocket and portaled to the diner's restroom. He'd been gone for a little less than five minutes, and as he returned to the table, he noted the dark-suited man in the corner who had the look of an FBI agent. He was careful not to make eye contact or reveal he'd noticed him as he sat down in time to receive his veggie and cheese omelet, with a pile of hash browns on top of it and a stack of pancakes on the side. The waitress set ketchup, hot sauce, and maple syrup in front of him, along with a carafe of coffee and a cola. He grinned. "You're the best, Sheila."

She nodded with a smile. "I know, but it's always good to hear it." The woman was matronly, older, a little chubby, with tight blonde hair piled on her head so it would stay out of her way while she worked. She lowered her voice and asked, "Friend of yours in the corner?"

He didn't look away from her. "Could be. Government likes to keep tabs on other parts of the government, you know. He been here long?"

"About five minutes after you."

"Impressive. Well, treat him decently. No need to poison him, this time. But be sure to keep our options open."

She laughed and turned away. He busied himself with food in front of him and mulled what he'd found on the flash drive in his mind. Only one conclusion emerged from his review, and he didn't like it at all.

Finley wouldn't have been so secretive about handing it over if that's all that was on the flash drive. I mean, I have clearance for most of that stuff. So it must hold something more, something he was worried about sharing. Guess this will be a project for Kayleigh and Deacon.

CHAPTER FIVE

Rath slotted weighted sticks into the sheaths that normally held his knives. Kayleigh had 3D printed the items for him, and they were about the same size and weight as his throwing blades. Plus, they had sensors on the base and the point so he'd know which end struck and so the computer systems could allocate damage accordingly.

The rest of his outfit was the team's standard practice gear, reduced to adjust for his smaller stature. It consisted of a vest and sleeves with impact sensors, legs the same, and his custom display goggles. The training suits were special in that they mimicked damage taken by locking up enough to hamper motion or freezing entirely to take someone out of the fight.

Around him, his partners for the session were donning their gear. Cara was closest to him and had chosen no replacements for her artifact daggers, instead preferring the pistols on her thighs and a rifle dangling from the strap attached to her shoulder. She wore the gloves and boots that they all did, also wired to sense impact locations and intensity.

Tony and Anik filled out the group. The former detective carried mismatched pistols, the team's standard Glock 17 in his left holster and a Desert Eagle in the other. All the weapons were training replicas, naturally, operating exactly like their real ones but discharging laser light instead. They even ejected shells, where appropriate, because early runs had revealed that some of the agents unconsciously used the falling shells as an aid to keep track of how many rounds they had left. It was a small thing, but small things mattered in combat. *Sometimes they matter more than anything. And I should know because I'm small.* He laughed to himself and asked, "Are we ready?"

Anik Khan finished attaching grenade canisters to a bandolier that ran across his chest and nodded. The small scars that covered one side of his face stood out on his tan skin. "Good here."

Cara and Tony confirmed they were ready as well. Tony continued, "I'll partner with Rath for the first run, so you lovebirds can have some quality time together." The other two responded with matching groans, while Rath laughed and made kissing noises like he did whenever people on the team dating came up.

Cara growled, "Just hit the button."

Rath shouted, "I'll do it," and jumped up on the bench that ran in front of the lockers. He ran along it and leapt, somersaulting twice in the air before slapping his hand on a large red button set next to a computer control panel. He landed cleanly as the room started to move.

Technically, it wasn't the room that moved. The

chamber they occupied was a cavernous rectangle, easily a football field in one direction and about a third of that in the other. One end of it held weights and exercise machines, along with lockers and some other incidentals. A series of cubes, a foot on each side, filled much of the rest of it. A flurry of computer arms mounted on the walls and the ceilings could arrange in any structure they requested.

The objects had been stacked on the back wall, occupying about half of the room's area, when they'd entered. Now, as they watched, the system created walls and ceilings, stairs, and corners. Occasionally, doors would slide down, gathered from a storage area in the rear, and destined for destruction in one way or another.

It took somewhere between five and ten minutes for the system to complete the process. Rath lost track of time, entranced by how the arms all worked together to create the training space. It was a ridiculously sophisticated piece of technology, an upgrade from the unit they'd had in Pittsburgh, which had used autonomous forklifts to move the cubes, taking far longer.

Kayleigh complained that this one was far more apt to break down, that it cost her and Hank way too much time in maintenance and repair. Still, improved efficiency meant they could create more complicated structures in less time. And time was a vital concern these days, as they ran around the country and the world looking for Rhazdon artifacts. *Finding opportunities to train is non-negotiable.*

Anik and Cara disappeared into one of the three entrance hallways the computer had created. The team's standard rule was to give the enemy five minutes to set up, then move in.

Rath's goal for this training session was to practice working with different partners. Most of the time he was at Diana's side or acting alone. Solo missions made sense, given his skills and ability to take care of himself by growing larger.

He'd taken the relocation to the vimana and the fact they all pretty much lived their jobs now as an opportunity to improve himself. He missed being able to go out to restaurants together, missed the backyard picnics they'd shared. The current blending of work and life got a little dull sometimes, which he thought was why they'd been out on so many missions lately. *Diana's bored too. She's just channeling it differently.*

Tony interrupted his musings by asking, "Want me to lead?"

Rath nodded. "Cara. Very dangerous. You go first."

The agent laughed. "Will do, partner. I'm counting on seeing your daggers fly by me while I'm busy diving to the ground to avoid getting shot."

The troll chuckled. "Of course."

Tony pulled each of his pistols from their holsters in sequence, checking them over like he would before going into battle in the field. Rath did the same with his weapons, touching the hilts of each knife substitute and verifying his batons were ready to be drawn from their holders. Those were identical to his usual ones but with a sensor tip instead of a stun one. The computer would add a virtual sizzle to any strike that hit properly. His partner said, "Okay, let's do it," then activated his comm and continued, "Stark and Rambo, beginning simulation."

Cara replied, "Croft and Khan, same."

Kayleigh, who would be keeping an eye on their efforts from her office, said, "Acknowledged. Rambo, don't give them too much make-out time. They both fight better when they're a little on edge."

Rath giggled. "Will do, Glam." The tech loved teasing everybody about everything, and he was totally on board with that behavior. He followed Tony as they moved through the middle corridor, which wasn't the one their opponents had chosen. It was impossible to know what traps they'd brought or improvised along the way. The one odd note that jarred the senses was the unnatural uniformity of the place, the one by one by one cubes making it look like they were walking in a huge Lego maze or something.

He stayed loose and limber, ready to move fast at the slightest provocation. Tony stopped. "Room ahead. An exit corridor continues directly opposite this one. Could be a four-way, could be anything. Definitely a decent site for an ambush. We can handle it one of two ways, as I see it. Dash in together and roll with whatever we find, or one goes in first as a decoy, with the other following. What's your preference?"

Rath thought the man sounded like a teacher and laughed at the mental image of him standing in front of a classroom full of small children. After a moment's consideration, he replied, "Together."

Tony nodded. "My choice too, partner." He drew his pistols. "I'll enter and go directly left, with my back to the wall. You do the same on the right. Ranged attacks at anything that's waiting for us. Then, if you feel the need to smack some people with your batons, let me know, and I'll cover you."

"Got it."

His partner counted down, and they burst into the room, ready for anything, only to find it empty. The agent chuckled. "Yep, that's what I love about training. Lots of stress that turns out to be nothing." While he was speaking, though, he gestured with his gun, bringing it up to his eyes and pointing to the hallway to his left. Then he gestured at Rath and the hallway to the right.

He nodded his understanding and made sure his grip on the knives he held was good. They both moved forward to the middle of the room and peered down the hallways that entered left and right. They were empty, as well. Tony said, "So, they skipped the easy ambush. Hell, maybe they *are* in the back making out or something. Jerks."

Rath laughed again. Their opposing force would never do anything so unprofessional, and everyone knew it. It was simply an amusing way to pass the time and relax the nerves. They continued onward, moving through several more rooms, some with additional hallways, some not. Then they came to a spot with a pair of staircases, one to the left, one to the right, each with a ninety-degree turn to continue going in the same direction but higher up. Rath said, "I go right, you go left?"

"Can't support each other that way. Quit being a loose cannon, Rambo." The troll snorted but grinned widely. It was a standing joke between them, the standard line from so many cop shows made all the better because his partner had been one. "So, we'll go up to the left. I'll lead. You guard my back. You know, you should think about carrying a gun."

"Knives and batons are good enough for me. Sometimes grenades."

Tony ascended the stairs and peeked his head around the corner, then continued upward. "Still. Not a bad skill to develop. I could spend some time with you on the range. That way, even if you didn't want to use one, you'd have the skills."

"That's a deal. Knife training in exchange?"

His partner shrugged. "I'll never be as good as you, but sure. Fair play. If you're going to learn a new skill, I should practice what I preach and learn one, too."

They stepped around another corner to find that the corridor widened before them, opening onto a room filled with columns and short walls. They retreated, and Rath observed, "Too good to pass up."

Tony said, "Agreed. So, here's what we'll do. We go in, and both go left. I lead, with you a step or two after. Since there are two of them, they'll probably try to attack from in front and behind. I'll take the front. The back is yours. Don't let yourself get distracted. They'll have something unique planned, I'm sure."

Rath nodded. "Got it. Ready." He held his knives loosely in his hands, prepared to throw.

"Moving." Tony flowed forward, with Rath trailing. He moved to the left, and they ran around the first pillar they came to, staying toward the outside of the room. Cara appeared ahead, popping up from behind a barrier shooting. Tony flinched, ducking and stepping to the side at the sight of her, and the bullets missed.

An instant later, flash-bang grenades went off. Tony cried out, clearly caught by the unexpected delay in their deployment—normally, the agents led with flash-bangs and used firearms after. Rath was obeying the instructions Tony had given him, carefully not looking forward and watching their rear, so he was ready when Anik stepped out from behind a different column with his gun raised.

His knives were on the way before the other man could finish aiming, and while his foe managed to squeeze off one shot that caught Rath in the shoulder, an area protected by his vest, his blades struck true, hitting the other agent's chest right above where the ceramic plates that reinforced their gear ended. The strike would've broken a collarbone, maybe, or cut into something vital in the zone between the chest and neck.

The computer must've judged it fatal because his opponent fell to the floor. Unfortunately, Tony did the same an instant later as gunfire sounded. His yelp cut off as the system rendered him functionally dead for the rest of the scenario. On his own again, Rath charged, giving the impression that he would go around the four-foot wall that separated him from Cara's position. Instead, though, he launched himself over it in a somersault, more knives already in his hands, ready to throw.

Cara was waiting with her pistols trained right on the spot where he'd jumped. His suit locked up and he slammed to the floor, hard enough that he would probably have at least one bruise from it. She walked over to him, shaking her head. "Predictable, buddy. Might've worked against someone who doesn't know you, but for someone who does? It's almost a guarantee that you'd come up and over rather than taking the long way."

"Next time, we'll do better. I'll be back."

She laughed and extended a hand to him. "I never doubted it for a second, my friend. Let's reset this thing and mix up the teams. I want you on my side for the next one."

CHAPTER SIX

D iana put the finishing touches on her makeup and rose to stand in front of the full-length mirror in her quarters. She'd turned the relatively bare-bones room into something fairly comfortable in the months they'd been in the vimana, although it still conveyed the vague feel of living in an industrial space. *Which, to be fair, is a solid step up from a lot of places I've lived.*

She smoothed the bright red dress that hugged her curves tightly enough that she wouldn't be able to carry any obvious weapons. Her boots had throwing knives on the sides and a stiletto down the back. The ensemble was too confining for the pair with the hideaway holster she would've chosen. She'd swept her hair away from her face, and her makeup was somewhere on the line between evening out and punk rock.

She always wanted to look a bit beyond the ordinary for her dates with Bryant, for her enjoyment, and because he seemed to enjoy it. A black clutch purse to match her boots was home to her backup Sig Sauer P238 pistol. It was loaded with seven anti-magic rounds, naturally.

Her illusion detection bracelet was fashionable enough for the outfit, gracing her right wrist, and the virtually invisible earpiece that served as the team's communication device remained tucked into her ear. She said, "Sheen, leaving the facility for D.C."

The baritone of the base's AI, which Rath had naturally named after Bruce Wayne's butler, responded, "Affirmative, Diana. Enjoy your date."

She grinned and replied, "Thank you, Alfred." Putting Kayleigh and Rath together with Deacon to work on the team's artificial intelligences had seemed like a good idea at first, giving the troll one more thing to learn. In retrospect, the personalities of their virtual comrades were becoming more and more prominent and potentially problematic as time went by. *I already have enough wacko people to manage. I don't need synthetic challenges as well.*

She opened a portal and stepped through to the backyard of the home she'd once owned in Washington. Her best friend, Lisa, occupied it now. They'd worked out a pay-to-own thing that was in the hands of a trust. Diana didn't need the extra income since her living expenses were nonexistent, so the money went back to her parents, who'd given her the house in the first place.

She wished she'd made some time to catch up with her friend, but Lisa was always busy with lawyer things. She'd changed to a different law firm when her previous one had started acting sketchy and was focusing on the grind of impressing the other partners.

Diana still had in the back of her mind the possibility of

turning her organization into a full investigative unit and adding Lisa to it as their legal eagle and team conscience. That was a down-the-road plan once they'd wrapped up the seemingly endless challenge of the Rhazdon artifacts.

She summoned a car and rode in the back. The driver-less vehicle took her to the trendy part of the city, stopping in front of the new restaurant Bryant had pulled some serious strings to get them into. The door opened for her automatically. As she stepped out, her date materialized at her side as if by magic. *Well, he's a wizard, so technically, it could be magic, but doubtful.*

Her boyfriend gave her the smile that made her stomach flutter sometimes, like tonight. "Hello, gorgeous. I was waiting for my girlfriend, but I think I need to ditch her and spend the night with you instead."

Diana returned a mock frown. "You're going to be spending the night on the couch if you keep up that nonsense, mister."

He laughed and swept her into a hug, which she returned enthusiastically. She'd never been as connected to any romantic partner as she was to Bryant, and the time their careers forced them to spend apart hadn't damaged that bond at all. *I guess we're polyamorous. Dating each other, dating our jobs. Kinky.* She broke his hold and pushed him gently away. "I'm starving, by the way, so if this is those places that think a serving is a tiny cube on a big dish or something, you're a dead man."

He grinned. "Please. I know you better than that. You're going to love it."

The door opened as they approached, held for them by a tuxedoed Asian gentleman. The interior was a harsh transition from the real world, and Diana stopped to take in her surroundings. A long bar that was a giant fish tank ran along one wall of the place. Patrons sat on stools, and between and around their legs, Diana spotted brightly colored fish darting to and fro. The exclusively female bartenders wore evening gowns, and their heavily painted faces made them look more like performers than servers.

The table arrangements in the dining room were in no order she could understand. They didn't follow the walls. They didn't follow each other, and they didn't match in angles or sizes. She said, "This place is chaos."

Bryant laughed as he nodded. "You're not wrong. Apparently, it's some new understanding of Feng Shui. They organized the furniture to bring prosperity to the location and to everyone who comes into it."

"Which is why the restaurant's name is Avarice?"

"Your brilliance never fails to amaze, love."

She poked him in the kidney as Bryant exchanged words with the host, another tuxedoed man, this one thin, blonde, and probably American, based on his looks. He led them through the maze of tables to one in the corner, with a pillar at the back of one of the two seats and only tables behind the other. She said, "Did your recon, huh?"

Bryant pulled out a chair for her. "Always. I want you to feel comfortable and relaxed so you're an easier mark. That's why you get the seat next to the column." They both shared a desire to have sightlines on any angle an enemy might use to come at them, but Diana's need for the defensive position was usually greater.

Or my paranoia. Whatever. She sat and said, "What, we don't get menus?"

He shook his head as he took his seat. "Everyone gets the same thing. They have a couple of nights a month where they'll take orders, but this isn't one of them."

She reached across the table to take his hand. "If this sucks, you're sleeping on the couch."

"Like you'd miss the chance to get some of this." His other hand gestured at himself. She had to admit, he cut a fine figure in his suit and tie, and the round glasses gave him sort of an Indiana Jones vibe. She retorted, "Oh, I'll still get that. But afterward, it's the couch for you."

He laughed and held his reply as the first course appeared in front of them. It was sushi, three pieces each. The waiter explained they were tuna, unagi, and lobster, then vanished. Accompanying the three reasonably sized cakes of rice topped with fish were three tiny bowls, each filled with a different sauce. After the first bite, she knew Bryant had chosen well. *Not that I'm going to tell him that. He's smug enough as it is.* Instead, she said, "How's work?"

He chewed and swallowed, then replied, "Problematic."

Diana's brain kicked into work mode, and she scanned the surroundings automatically as she replied, without changing her tone, "Oh, in what way?"

"I hear there's some concern about your team." While he spoke, his fingers made signals for surveillance. She nodded, having already spotted a suspicious man out in the street leaning against a lamppost, pretending to wait for a car. For all she knew, there could be others in the restaurant, although he'd probably chosen such an exclusive place deliberately to ensure they'd at least have a modicum of privacy for their meal. *We'll have to check the hotel room thoroughly when we get there.*

They always rented a hotel room for their date nights, feeling like it made the whole thing a little more special, but followed no particular pattern in selecting the hotels. So, again, the likelihood that the room would be compromised was low, but they had to assume it was always non-zero. "Oh really? Say more."

He chuckled and waited while the waiter exchanged their dishes for another round of sushi, this time with Kobe beef, teriyaki chicken, and some bright red meat she couldn't identify. Again, a trio of sauces accompanied them, and again, they were outstanding. "There's some suspicion that the quantity of artifacts you're turning over doesn't justify your team's existence or some such thing."

She frowned. "Who's counting?"

His tone stayed light while his eyes, meeting hers, conveyed his concern. "No idea. That wasn't part of the information I received."

"You trust the person who clued you in?"

Bryant nodded. "Completely."

Diana paused to eat the mystery chicken and decided it was tandoori. "I thought the government's position was that they were going to trust us to do our thing. Wasn't that the deal?"

"There's trust, and there's *trust*. Apparently, they're only willing to go so far. Or maybe a secret shakeup occurred and someone new is in charge somewhere. You know how the government is."

She laughed. "Impractical? Inefficient?"

Bryant swallowed and patted his lips with a napkin. "True on all counts. Anyway, I thought you should know.

Maybe we can skip the work talk for the rest of the meal, huh?"

His words sent a thrill of alarm through her. Normally, the meal *was* when they talked about work, so they could focus on other things once they made it to the hotel room. *This might be worse than he's letting on.* Instead, she smiled and nodded. "Sure, Bry-Bry. Anything that makes you happy."

Several hours later, Bryant fell back into their sweaty sheets beside her with a loud exhale. Diana waited for her breathing to return to normal, then snuggled up against him. They'd checked the place thoroughly for bugs and had put countersurveillance devices on every wall to ensure sound waves wouldn't travel through them to be detected by microphones. They were as safe as they were going to get. Still, she put her mouth right next to his ear before demanding, "Okay, spill."

He rolled over to face her and spoke in a voice that wouldn't have carried more than a foot past her. "I have a flash drive for you. It holds a bunch of research on you and your team."

She frowned. "Like someone's investigating us?"

Bryant gave a small nod. "That's my guess. What I was able to access were normal files, but the fact that they're collected together seems like something worth being worried about. I'm guessing there's more to it. My contact wouldn't have taken the risk of passing this to me if there wasn't."

Diana sighed at the prospect of their date ending early. "Would you call this an 'existential, get on it right now,' kind of crisis?"

He shook his head. "No, I'd call it a 'let's spend the night exhausting each other since if this is a problem, we don't know when we'll be together again' kind of crisis."

She laughed, pushed him down on his back, and threw one leg over his stomach. "Well then, we better not waste any time."

CHAPTER SEVEN

Diana was up before dawn the next day, as she always was. She gave Bryant a lengthy goodbye kiss, then portaled back to the base. A quick shower brought her to full consciousness, and she shoved some food into her face and filled her largest travel mug with strong coffee, sensing the day ahead would be one that would require the extra energy. She paused, considering, then dumped a couple of packets of sugar in as well. *Going to need every boost I can get, probably.*

She was waiting impatiently when Kayleigh and Deacon showed up, arriving together doubtless after sharing breakfast. *And maybe the same bed before that.* Diana didn't judge and carefully stayed unaware of exactly what romantic arrangements her people were making while stuck in the vimana. As long as they continued to do their jobs properly, she was fine with whatever. *One more way my rules are different from what the government would have us do, I guess. Besides, it would be rather hypocritical of me to take a stand against it.*

Her inner voice offered, "Probably won't be as easy to explain the whole 'not handing over magical items and artifacts' thing, though."

Shut it. From the moment she'd taken charge of the team, she'd done things her way, and she had no plans to change that approach. Rules were all well and good, and she followed most of them. But the exigencies of being in the field simply overrode some of the guidelines her nominal superiors had imposed. *One of those is the need to understand these artifacts better and figure out how to use them against our enemies without getting compromised in the process. Which we can't do if we hand them all over.*

Kayleigh stepped to her side and frowned. The tech's blonde hair was in pigtails, a style she'd used even before Margot Robbie made it popular in *Suicide Squad*. Her tone was filled with sarcasm as she said, "Well, you look grimmer than normal. How lovely that you decided to grace us with your dour presence right at the start of our day."

Deacon laughed. He was in a Spider-Man T-shirt and jeans. He'd lost weight since joining them, the peer pressure of all the agents' physical routines eventually wearing down his resistance until he felt compelled to join in. Kayleigh, too. Neither would win any bodybuilding competitions, but they were both fitter and healthier than before.

Given the lack of social options here in Antarctica, exercise becomes far more appealing. Diana shook her head, not smiling at Kayleigh's dig. "I have work for you guys. Breaking the encryption on a flash drive."

Deacon said, "My rig can handle it, whatever it is. Hand it over with all speed."

Diana cautioned, "This thing could have malware. Might try to send out a signal, or whatever."

The infomancer rolled his eyes. "Boss, handling toxic programs *is* my kung fu. And it is strong."

She frowned. "I recognize that."

Rath, who had crept in quietly behind her, a game he often liked to play to her detriment, said, "*The Core*. Come on, that one was easy."

Diana twisted and scowled at her partner. "We can't all watch movies all the time. Some of us have to work."

Kayleigh replied, "So that's what you call sleeping with Bryant? Work? I mean, I can see where it could be. He strikes me as the demanding type."

She flipped the tech off with one hand while Deacon plucked the flash drive out of the other. He said, "We don't need you for this, Kitana. Go cause trouble elsewhere."

Diana laughed. "Oooh, burn."

Kayleigh responded with a theatrical scowl. "He'll pay. You'll pay. *Everyone* will pay. Except Rath, he's the only nice one around here. Hey buddy, help me make them all pay?"

The troll grinned and raced to the tech's side. "You know it."

Diana shook her head and followed Deacon into his work area. A huge desk supporting lots of monitors, multiple keyboards, a mouse, some other interface devices, and several things she didn't recognize at all greeted her. A chair set in the center of it, a large expensive one she'd bought out of her pocket, knowing how much time he'd wind up spending in it as their sole computer expert.

Small opened bags of salty snacks and many cans of soda, also opened, littered the table behind his workstation. He detoured to a beverage cooler in the corner and pulled out a six-pack of Dr. Pepper, cracking one as he sat in his seat and depositing the others on the table. She sat in one of the two chairs at the table and watched as code flew on the big screen in the center.

A folder popped up, and he poked through it quickly, finding personnel files, blueprints of the vimana and other ARES installations, and other similar data. She muttered, only loud enough that Deacon would be able to hear, "I see what Bryant was talking about. That's a lot of stuff, but none of it is particularly secret."

He nodded. "Yeah. Also, the schematics for this room don't include the changes we've made. Maybe they don't care about small alterations, or maybe they don't know. Can't be sure, either way."

She frowned, knowing she shouldn't ask but equally certain that she had to, to be positive. "No one could have gotten into your systems, right?"

"I'm going to pretend you didn't ask such a stupid question because the shame you would feel would doubtless overwhelm your entire mind and render you useless." He hit some buttons. "Okay, I'm sending in my cracking team. Let's see what's hiding on this flash drive."

The way he described his interface with the computer always intrigued her. Diana could never sense his magic at work like she did some other magics but knew he was using it whenever he interacted with a computer, even with his smartphone. It was as natural to him as breathing, as he'd explained.

She couldn't conceive of what it would be like to be an infomancer but was deeply glad Kayleigh had identified her online gaming partner as a potential member of the team. He'd been nothing short of indispensable from the day he joined.

A few moments later, a new series of folders replaced the visual on the screen, each labeled with only a number. Deacon said, "Okay, now we're into something useful. You were right. A cute little virus was attached to it. At the moment, it's in a tiny cyber box, bashing itself against the walls and trying to contact the outside world. Maybe later I'll take it apart and see if we can turn it against the senders."

"Well done."

He shrugged. "I am what I am, and in this case, it's a white-hot white hat hacker." He opened the first folder, and a picture of a young, redhead, pale-skinned woman popped up.

Diana frowned, moving from irritated to angry. "Why the hell do they have records about Cali?" Diana and her team had helped the woman on several occasions, but not on anything that should've caught the government's attention. "As far as I know, she's in New Atlantis, being the head of her house or whatever, right?"

Deacon nodded. "Yeah. As of our last regular check-in, that's still true." The screen showed a series of dates and locations. "This has records of most of the times someone from the team engaged with her. *Including* the check-ins." His tone turned darker. "How the hell do they have that information?"

Diana shook her head. "No telling. But we need to find

out. Keep looking." The second folder had detailed reviews of all the missions her unit had undertaken, from their inception up to the previous week's operations. "Okay, I'm officially starting to get pissed off. This is directed only at us, right? There aren't any deep research records of the other ARES units' ops?"

He flicked through the rest of the documents in that folder and confirmed her suspicion. She leaned back with a sigh. "I'm almost afraid to find out what's in the next one."

Deacon replied, "Right there with you, boss." Nonetheless, he opened the next folder, and more personnel files popped up.

"Of course. Ruby, Alejo, and the costumes in Magic City. Should've figured."

The infomancer nodded. "Apparently, we're like typhoid Mary for the government surveillance teams. Look, these records have entries after we last did anything in Magic City. Looks as if things have stabilized a bit there, anyway."

Diana slapped her hands on the table in anger. "I do not like the idea that people are watching us. I *really* don't like the idea that they're watching us hard enough that the surveillance is spreading to our friends and contacts. We're going to have to figure out a way to put out the word, quietly, and let everyone know they're under the government's eye."

While she'd been talking, Deacon had been loading up another folder, and the document that arrived on the screen took her breath away. The infomancer said, "Oh, shit," and magnified it to fill the entire display.

"You've got that right." In front of her was a list of

options for "dealing" with her and her team. First on the list was a change in leadership, firing both her and Bryant and replacing them with others. The document referenced "Tier one" but didn't explain what that meant.

The second option was rolling all of ARES into the existing FBI structure, with lots of oversight, essentially demoting both her and Bryant and putting others in charge of them, with the same arrangement for the other bureaus. *That's not going to happen. I'll walk before I work for some government chucklehead. Other than Bryant, that is.*

The third item was the most alarming one. It recommended disbanding the team entirely but also referenced criminal proceedings against its members. "Damn. Somebody really doesn't like us."

The infomancer replied, "Everyone likes me, so it must be you, Boss."

Deacon's joke, which easily could have come out of Kayleigh's mouth, given the similarity in their humor styles, fell flat. Diana stood with a growl. "None of those options works for me. Especially the last one. They'll initiate criminal proceedings against anyone on this team over my dead body. I mean that literally. Figure out who's behind this garbage and what their endgame is. And I need that information yesterday. Get to it."

CHAPTER EIGHT

Deacon sighed and pushed himself back from the computer keyboards, reaching blindly behind him for his soda. The first can he found was empty. The second one was as well, and he turned with an annoyed grunt to find that the entire dozen he'd put on the table were empty. He didn't know why his magic jacked up his metabolism so intensely when he was spending time inside the magical web or his systems, but he was equally starving and parched.

He stood with a groan, muscles protesting the fact that he'd been sitting in the chair for something like eight hours without a break, and headed for the canteen. Along the way, he commed Kayleigh, who met him there. She said, "What's up, working man?"

He rolled his neck and winced at the cracking sound it made. "I'm getting too old for this."

She laughed. "Please. Compared to the dinosaurs around here, we're newborns."

"Anyway, I think I'm good to go. Been making sure all

my systems are sharp, and all my programs are as ready as they can be. Want to ride along?"

His girlfriend nodded. "You know I do. Far more entertaining than a night watching movies while you work."

He made a face at her. "Yeah, the real-world danger involved makes it more amusing, right?"

She treated his comment as serious, even though he hadn't meant it that way. "Absolutely. Still, it's not like you're going to die in there or anything."

"No," he agreed. "But, if I let anyone get into our systems, Diana will murder me, so it's pretty much the same thing."

"Good point. For the record, I'm a spectator. If she comes in with guns blazing, I am *not* involved."

Deacon laughed. "That's what I like in a partner. True loyalty."

Kayleigh smacked him on the arm. "You knew what you were getting with me when you signed up. How many times did I use you as cannon fodder playing online?"

"Pretty much all of them, if I recall properly." He grabbed several wrapped sandwiches, a large bag of chips, and one of the ever-present carafes of coffee, then turned to leave. "Before you ask, this is all for me. Get your own food, leech."

She laughed. "Chivalry is alive and well in Antarctica, ladies."

A half-hour later, he was fed, hydrated, and seated behind his computers, ready to go. Kayleigh sat on the gaming chair she'd pulled in from her workspace, with her feet extended in front of her on the built-in rest. A glance at the camera that displayed what he referred to as his "meat space" when he was present in the virtual showed she had the VR rig on.

Unlike setups with only goggles, this one had a full face covering that added sensory input appropriate to the scenario. Larger and more complicated suits existed, and they had one in the workshop to play with, but since they weren't using an interface she could interact with, it didn't make sense to spend the bandwidth on an increased connection.

As if she was reading his mind, Kayleigh said, "It's great to ride along and all, but I wish I could help."

Deacon paused for a second, considering it. "You know, I wonder if that might be doable. My magic is pretty strong. Maybe it could make that link work fast enough that a full VR suit could allow you to function as if you were inside. It's worth checking out, but a question for another day, when Diana isn't sharpening her sword in anticipation of my failure." *With her, it's a* literal *sword, which adds an extra measure of pressure to the scale.*

He turned his attention back to his loading screen, positioned his hands over the keyboard, and extended magic into the system, funneled through the wand he wore around his wrist as a bracelet. "Here we go."

The initial sensation was like falling, dropping from the sky without a parachute toward whatever mystery lay below. An interplay between his desires and the system he was targeting would determine the personality of the virtual environment. In this case, it was a government server he shouldn't have the address of, much less any chance of accessing.

Diana had been good to him. Since he'd joined the

team, every time she or Bryant had gone into any government building, their electronics had been gathering data, reams and reams of ones and zeros. When he wasn't actively using his systems, they worked on that information, sifting and parsing it for any useful tidbits it might hold. It had provided his initial clue to the existence of this server, pulled from a conversation between IT personnel as Bryant had walked past them.

Once he had that first piece, he'd put his artificial intelligences on the lookout for ways in. They'd found one through a vendor that produced reporting software and hadn't properly upped their security on the day of a new update. His bots had entered and created a foothold, nothing more than a path to the server, but it was enough.

I'll do the rest. He landed, his avatar finishing with the Ironman superhero pose. Kayleigh materialized standing beside him. His main view was first person, but a window off to the side of his visual field held a third-person view, and he saw that his character wore a cowled cloak, with black leather armor underneath and Middle Ages weapons on his belt.

He turned in a full circle, examining the scene. "Cool. *Dishonored.* I've been playing a lot lately, and I guess my subconscious and the system found common ground there."

Kayleigh, whose avatar's outfit matched his, replied, "Is that the one with the swarms of rats?" Her voice held an obvious edge of distaste.

He grinned. "Yeah, but they're usually good guys. Anyway, here's the deal. The tower up there," he gestured, "is our destination. We'll have to move through the city without getting noticed, and if someone does spot us, they need to die before they can give the alarm."

"By *die*, you mean?"

"I need to kill them in the system. No big deal."

"By *people*, you mean?"

He laughed. "Most of the beings we'll see will be programs, ranging in sophistication from simple guard dog bots to actual artificial intelligences. It's not a ridiculous thought that an infomancer could be watching the place. Probably not more than one, and I doubt this would be their only gig, but we need to be aware of the possibility of advanced AIs and a magical human presence since this is the government. Who the hell knows what they're up to at any given moment, right?"

Kayleigh's avatar shrugged. "Right. Although you could say the same about our team, I think."

He didn't reply, only moved down the cobblestone street. Shops made up the left-hand side, and a large wall ran along the right. From playing the game, he knew an ocean or harbor lay on the other side of the wall, separated from it by a sandy expanse. He assumed the map would be similar to the ones he was familiar with, probably identical in fact, since it was his subconscious driving the illusion. However, the enemies, and the tricks and traps they might've left for him, wouldn't align with the game at all.

Deacon found his first problem when a guard dog—literally, a canine watching over the street—lifted its snout in his direction. He froze, calling up a concealment program that would blend him into the shadows of the wall. He'd already engaged camouflage programs to make his cloak match the surroundings, and it was voluminous enough that he could keep it wrapped around his armor.

His pistol crossbow climbed upward ever so slowly to point at the dog without alarming it. The weapon gave a muted *thwack* as it sent the projectile hurtling forward. The bolt caught the beast in the throat, dropping it. He moved ahead to conceal the body, but it pixelated suddenly and faded from existence. He muttered, "Oh, that's handy. Thank you, subconscious."

Kayleigh asked, "You can't simply make that happen?"

As his avatar continued forward, he replied, "No. I can't consciously set the rules of the environment. That would require a whole different kind of fight, and it's much more stand-up, force against force, than this sort of incursion, which only looks for weak spots to exploit."

"'Kay," she said, her standard response when she didn't understand what he was talking about but figured some kind of sound was necessary.

He laughed. "I'll explain it in more detail sometime."

Kayleigh rolled her eyes. "Next time I have insomnia, maybe."

"Witch."

"Bastard."

He grinned at the exchange of familiar insults, then stopped again. Ahead, two guards patrolled, both of them wearing armor similar to his but lacking the cloak. The one on the right held a torch, suggesting it was a specialized detection bot. His partner wielded dual crossbows, one in each hand, signaling it was the offensive member of the pair. *Doesn't matter which they are, they both need to go down together, so they can't shout an alarm.*

Another cloaking program wrapped him in silence as he moved stealthily forward, pausing six feet away from his foes. They still hadn't noticed him, which he considered lucky, given how close he'd managed to get. He transferred the crossbow to his left hand and drew his sword an inch at a time, as quietly as possible from its scabbard.

When it was free, he dashed behind the pair and shot the left one in the back of the neck with a bolt at point-blank range while he rammed the sword through the other's back, aiming for the heart. Both blows struck true, and the duo glittered into nothingness. "Yes. I am *invincible*."

Kayleigh snorted. "You remember what happened to the guy who said that in *Goldeneye*, right?"

"Yeah, but he was a boastful jerk. I'm the real thing."

"That's what he probably thought, too."

Around the next corner, he found a challenge he hadn't anticipated awaiting him. He released a sigh. "Great. They're having a party." The only route to his target ran across an arched wooden bridge and through a courtyard. Food and drink booths covered the span, with the space between them filled with drunk revelers in ornate masks wandering around.

Kayleigh's grin said it all, but she added to it with a wry comment. "See? You set up the universe like that, and the universe smacks you down."

CHAPTER NINE

His companion said, "I do love a party."

Deacon frowned at the press of bodies ahead. "Yeah, except this is almost certainly a party filled with enemies in disguise."

Kayleigh laughed. "You mean this isn't an online gathering of tech people who are too introverted and antisocial to meet in real life?"

"First, ow. Second, no. My systems are telling me that most or all of these are bots. There might be some infomancers hidden among them, or maybe even a lonely systems administrator participating as an avatar, but it's there as a defensive measure.

"Why?"

He was already scanning the sky, turning to look in all directions, and deploying countersurveillance programs. "Distraction. Confusion. Hang on a sec while my bots do their thing."

It was a few seconds before results flowed into his mind. In the real world, it was data scrolling past his eyes.

In the computer simulation, it was intuition and pattern recognition, his magic taking the information and transforming it into his character's feelings.

"Okay. The bridge itself is a trap. Sensors all over. They're trying to funnel intruders in a specific direction, which is why they built the place with only one obvious access. The party, at least on the bridge, is there to make us less likely to notice the other stuff."

Kayleigh nodded. "It's clever. You have to give them that."

"I don't have to give them anything. Jerks, all of them jerks." He inevitably fell into his character during missions, blending his personality with whatever his avatar was supposed to be.

In this case, he was an assassin. Serving the cause of justice in the end, sure, but not someone with any compunction about murder when killing was necessary. He'd played the game through in stealth mode, where the enemies lived, and in chaos mode, where every foe died in particularly bloody fashion.

This run against the government server presented similar choices. *I'll have to go hard eventually, but I'm not setting foot on that bridge.* He led Kayleigh back along the route of their approach.

As soon as they were out of the partygoers' line of sight, he climbed over the wall separating them from the beach and dropped stealthily down to the sand. His companion rippled into place beside him. She asked, "What's the plan, man?"

He lifted his hands, and climbing spikes glittered on them. Outside the simulation, his programs would be engaging the system's defenses, poking and prodding for weaknesses. They'd find him a path through and make sure the defenders were unable to detect his intrusion. "We pretend we're Spider-Man."

Kayleigh clapped. "Excellent. Rath is going to be upset that he missed this."

Deacon chuckled. "Well, when the new gaming console I bought him finally gets off back order, he'll have all the Spider-Man he wants." He strode forward to the underside of the bridge. Reaching up as far as he could, he used the climbing spikes to get a handhold, stabbing them deep into the mortar between the bricks. *If I tried this in the real world, likely the stuff would've crumbled, and I'd have an eyeful of dust.*

That wasn't a concern here since the whole thing was one giant metaphor. As long as the programs did their work, he would be fine. His climbing effort was the simulated representation of his fingers dancing across the keyboard and his mind adapting to the real-time situations his computer systems encountered.

He kicked up with one boot, which now had a large climbing spike attached. It stabbed into the mortar and held. He rammed in the points on the other hand, then, with a deep breath, the other boot. He was hanging at a slight backward angle from the arc that made up the start of the bridge.

That part wasn't hard. What *would* be difficult was crossing the river upside down without letting vertigo or the natural fear of being above water that probably held the computer equivalent of piranha and sharks get to him. He made his way slowly, remaining as silent as he could, given the need to stab metal into soft stone repeatedly. The distance to the opposite shore dwindled in a series of releases, stabs, and releases again, the pattern seeming endless as he focused on the actions.

Finally, he was close enough to the other side to drop to the ground. He'd traversed the bridge safely, which was cause for a slight celebration, but that was only the first part of the plan. Laughter from the courtyard above filtered down, and he shook his head. "Of all the nights to have a party."

Kayleigh, who'd been floating beside him during the transit and was now next to him on the rocky soil, replied, "The party would be every night, right? If it's a defensive tactic?"

"You're accurate, but you're also messing with the illusion. When inside the simulation, it's best to spend most of your time acting like it's real."

"Including complaining about things that aren't *actually* real?"

"Shut it." He concentrated for a moment, activating several programs he'd prepared against the need to hide in plain sight, and his clothes changed. His initial plan for the tower had been to go in disguised as a guard, but that would be more conspicuous than appearing as a random party guest. His leather armor and cloak disappeared, replaced by a fine velvet tunic and trousers. Polished shoes and a slouchy hat finished the look.

Kayleigh observed, "This game could use some serious fashion advice."

"Hush or I'll disconnect you." He planted a smile on his face and strode boldly toward the stairs that led upward. He passed guards along the way, nodding at them as if they were a lower rank than he was and as if he had every right to be in that place at that time. They didn't react, so he wasn't forced to use the daggers hidden inside his clothes.

Upon reaching the courtyard, he snagged a tankard from a table, pretended to drink from it, and milled around aimlessly. At least, that's how it would appear to anyone observing his actions. In reality, he'd refocused all of his programs on conquering the doorway that led into the tower and was killing time while they worked. The guards kept it locked, and he needed it not to be.

He was fully confident his bots could figure out the encryption and open the way but grew more nervous with each passing second that the door stayed closed. He sensed the guards taking an interest in him and continued to behave normally, joining a conversation with two other men who scowled at his approach but didn't otherwise react, too polite to tell him to go away.

Finally, he heard the *click* of the door's bolt sliding back, and he called upon a special program. Out above the water, fireworks suddenly burst into view, the sound of the explosions and the brilliant visual display capturing the attention of everyone at the party. He slipped inside the tower while they were distracted, and the door closed and locked behind him.

Its interior was far less impressive than its exterior. A rectangular staircase climbed along the outer walls. High above, it disappeared into the roof of the large open area, which was probably also the floor of another room. The information he wanted would doubtless be there. He said as much, and Kayleigh asked, "How do you know?"

He shrugged as he climbed the stairs, his outfit transforming back into the assassin's gear as he released the camouflage programs. "This whole thing is a metaphor for the computer system we're invading. We're after specific information, and no matter where it *actually* is in the real world, for us, it will be up in this tower since that's the central locale for the simulation. The number of stairs we have to climb probably connects to the difficulty my programs are having in getting us into it. The distance may change as we're walking."

His companion shook her head. "This is super weird. You know that? I knew you were odd, but this is pushing the boundaries, even for you."

He laughed. "Like you're one to talk." He drew his sword in his right hand and readied the pistol crossbow in his left. "Not sure what we're going to find at the top, but I'd guess it won't be friendly."

"Anything I can do?"

He chuckled. "Well, I'd tell you to be quiet while I deal with whatever is up there, but you asked about things you *can* do, and it's quite obvious silence isn't something you're physically capable of."

Kayleigh's avatar stuck her tongue out at him. "Har, har, har."

"See? Proof." The surrounding reality rippled suddenly, and when things reverted to normal, they were only a dozen steps away from their destination. He drew a deep breath and dashed up the final stairs, holding his sword in a high defensive position angled over his head.

His instincts proved their value once again as a descending blade clanged off his before he was fully in the room. Deacon dove aside and rolled to his feet in time to deflect another blow. He tried to bring his crossbow in line, but it flew from his hand as his opponent's second weapon slammed into it. He scowled. "Those swords are way too big for you to dual wield them with that musculature."

His foe, a slightly built woman in a geisha's outfit complete with the painted face, laughed. "Oh, but you're in *my* reality here."

Deacon shook his head. "Our reality." Reaching out with his magic, he grabbed the armor stand in the corner and threw it at her. The geisha danced nimbly aside in a whirl of skirts, and he took stock of his surroundings. The room seemed to be medieval Japan, complete with the paper walls and tapestries that were stereotypical of the setting. His opponent had a matched katana and tanto, both longer than they should be.

He summoned a new element to his costume, gauntlets with curved projections modeled after Christopher Nolan's *Batman* films. He used them to block her strikes, catching her off blade with one and giving a deft twist to send it flying away. Single sword against single sword, they marched back and forth across the space. She struck high, and he lifted his blade in defense. Her next attack was low, and he leapt over it with ease.

Deacon was devoting the first part of the battle to figuring out her style and saw a weakness immediately. While she was good with the swords, that was *all* she was good at with, suggesting the human on the other end either wasn't as skilled an infomancer as him or wasn't an info-mancer at all, but simply a defensive operative. He swung high to draw her blade upward, then snapped out a kick that caught her in the stomach.

She flew across the room, defying the laws of gravity, and smashed through one of the paper walls. A foot behind it was the tower's stone, and when she struck it, the sword fell from her hand. He reached out with his telekinesis and grabbed it before it hit the floor. He pulled it toward him, stopped it in midair, turned it, and hurled it back the way it had come. It impaled the geisha in the center of her torso, and she screamed in anger rather than pain as she pixilated and disappeared.

Kayleigh said, "What did you do?"

Deacon walked toward a small ornate box, like a tiny treasure chest, that rested on a pedestal along the wall to his left. "Disconnected the user from the system with an overflow of data. Basically, the same thing hackers use to knock out websites, but much more sophisticated." He opened the coffer and held up a cat statue, shining gold and covered in gemstones.

"That's it?"

He nodded. "That's it. Let's get out of here." He kicked the meat-space button under his desk that served as an emergency disconnect and leaned back in his chair with a sigh. His body hurt like it always did after such an episode. It wasn't as if he worked his muscles, but somehow his mind made it seem like he had.

He turned and cracked open a soda, drinking the entire thing down in a single guzzle. He opened another and sipped that one. When he'd lubricated his mouth enough to talk again, he said, "I think I'm going to have to find a new game for a while. That one has some harsh connotations now."

Kayleigh nodded as she pulled off the VR helmet. "I hear Candyland online is nice."

He laughed, the dissipating stress making it louder and longer than it should've been, given the stupidity of the joke. "Yeah, maybe I'll try that out."

"Should we wake the boss?"

He shook his head. "We have the data, but we still have to decrypt it. My bots will get to work on it. Should be ready sometime in the early morning." A yawn overtook him. "Now, time for even the invincible to sleep."

Kayleigh lifted an eyebrow. "Just sleep?"

He grinned at the beautiful woman that he still couldn't believe was willing to date him. "Well, if you have something better in mind, I'm certainly open to suggestions."

CHAPTER TEN

D iana stepped out of the shower and stared at herself in the bathroom's small mirror. *I'm not old enough to have those wrinkles at the corners of my eyes. Stupid job.* She headed out into her bedroom to get dressed, continuing to grumble mentally about work, life, all of it.

Her anger at discovering the government was keeping such a close eye on them, obviously with malicious intent, had sent her into a frenzy of training the night before. She'd pushed herself until exhaustion had claimed her, barely making it into her bunk before losing consciousness.

Today, she felt strangely hollow as a result, like she was a skin shell with a void inside it. It was better than holding all that anger within her, but she'd lost her sense of equilibrium. *I doubt I'm likely to regain it anytime soon. Every time I think of those bastards having surveillance on us, I want to grab someone by the throat and shake them until their head pops off.*

She sighed and grabbed her normal base outfit of beat-up tactical pants and a black tank with a well-worn button-down uniform shirt on top of it. This one sported the logo of Two Worlds Security, the company they'd run as a way to disguise their actions in Pittsburgh. *Different times.* Her last check-in on James Maxis and Vicki Greene, affectionately known to her team as Starsky and Hutch, had been positive.

Diana and Bryant had set up the company to be a real thing, tied to their presence but not part of it, and those two were handling its continuing operation well. They kept the profits, and she and her team earned a little off-the-books revenue by supplying them with the weapons, ammunition, and intelligence that made it all possible. The arrangement worked out for everyone. *Except, apparently, the government.* She sat down to pull on her most comfortable boots, her oldest pair with only a knife in each, the hilts sticking up a bit but covered by her loose pant cuffs.

She headed for the commissary and grabbed one of the large travel mugs full of coffee always ready in the morning and a pair of breakfast sandwiches from a warming tray. Local supply was nonexistent in Antarctica, so someone made a grocery run each week, stocking up on the essentials. Her team members rotated preparing food, cleaning, and the other chores that kept the place running. She stayed out of it, except to say that no, she wasn't going to take a turn. Yes, she understood that might be annoying to them, and no, she didn't really care.

She arrived at her office door as Cara did. The other woman looked perfectly put together, right down to her subtly flawless cosmetics, making Diana rethink her decision not to dry her hair. *Screw it. I'm tired. I get a break.* Her subordinate said, "Morning, boss. Seemed like you were going pretty hard yesterday."

She nodded. "Yeah, we need to talk." She opened the door and walked inside. "Close that behind you and have a seat." Cara complied. "It appears we have some opposition somewhere in the government."

Cara frowned. "Like a pissed-off senator or something?" They'd faced a lot of that in the early days of their organization.

Diana shrugged and sipped her coffee. "No telling, but from the amount of data they gathered, it's an operation with some people and tech behind it. That argues against 'just' a senator. Maybe a senator with some connections in operations."

"Military?"

"No idea. Could be. Could be the FBI. Hell, it could be another organization like ours that we haven't heard about. Can't trust those political bastards."

Cara chuckled. "You know, it might be that attitude that's caused people not to like us, assuming someone saw through your always-pleasant exterior."

Diana scowled. "I'm aware."

Her comm chimed, and she held up a finger as Deacon's voice came into her ear. "Boss, that file is done decrypting. I haven't opened it, but it's clean and ready for you on your private drive."

"Thanks." She pressed her index finger against a drawer of her desk, activating the biometric lock. The drawer slid open, and she took her heavy-duty laptop out and opened it. "Deacon did some digging. Let's find out what he came up with."

She turned the computer so Cara could see the screen as well and hit the requisite buttons. A list of names popped up, and she searched their databases to find out who they were. "Wow. We've managed to get members of both parties to dislike us?"

Cara laughed. "Look at that, boss. You've inspired people who probably hate each other to work together. Nicely done."

Diana scrolled past the information on the senators from Nevada, one a Republican, one a Democrat. The next several names in the file were FBI. "Really, the feebies almost had to be involved."

Cara nodded. "No military. That's good, anyway."

She frowned. "This Kevin Serrano here. We have no records on him."

"Like he's new?"

"I guess that's possible. Or his files have been scrubbed." The next record was labeled Tier one, and upon opening revealed a dozen names alongside their personnel files. Diana breathed, "Holy hell. Top people at the CIA, Treasury, FBI."

Cara pointed at one. "And Army military police. Wow. The best of the best of the best, like in *Men in Black*."

She stared daggers at her subordinate. "Honestly, if you people don't quit it with the movie quotes, I'm going to start shooting anyone who does it in the foot."

The other woman snorted. "Like you could shoot Rath."

"He gets a sleep dart." They didn't have sleep darts, but

their intel said that Ruby had used them in Magic City, and she was sure she could borrow a few from the other woman. *She owes me at least that much, not that she'd refuse even if she didn't.*

Cara reached over and clicked something on the laptop, the information summoning a frown even bigger than Diana's. "What the hell is this? A military version of the AET makes total sense and has been in the works for some time, but this setup looks like it's for urban deployment, not fights in the field."

As they reviewed the files, it became increasingly clear the government was spinning up several operations either aimed at them or intended to do the things that her team did. When taken as a whole, it didn't paint a good picture.

Diana growled, "Okay. Now that we know who these scumbags are, we need to take them on rather than letting them play their games."

"Agreed."

"On the political side, I'll ask Bryant to chat with the people he knows, see if he can get a hint of who's at the top of this dung heap. Maybe it's the mystery man. Once we have a target, we can figure out how to deal with him or her."

Cara replied, "On the operational side, we'll need to boost our countersurveillance actions since Bryant thinks they're watching us. Given the information here, he's probably right."

Diana nodded. "They're watching. I'll send you the rest of the data when we finish here."

"Perfect. I'll get with Kayleigh, work up some more

drone coverage for field ops. Anything on the immediate radar?"

"Italy. Venice, I think. Some chucklehead who apparently found a Rhazdon artifact in a museum, and instead of being a good upstanding citizen and turning it in to Interpol, has decided to sell it on the black market."

Cara rolled her eyes, clearly sharing Diana's opinion of the man. "Sending Sloan in to buy it?"

"We're low on funds for that sort of thing. I was considering requesting more, but this information pretty well kills that notion. No, you all will have to go in and take it."

Her subordinate shrugged. "Not a problem. Timeframe?"

"We have some leeway since he's working the buyers to get more from the sale. Maybe start some recon today."

"Will do."

She considered suggesting to Cara that they should find a backup location for the most precious items in their artifact storage, given what they'd learned. *No telling what limits these bastards might have.*

Suddenly, a shrill staccato alarm blasted out of the speakers mounted in the ceiling. It took her a moment to remember what that particular cadence meant, and she and Cara said simultaneously, in a similar tone of disbelief, "Intruders." Diana snapped, "Alfred, status."

The base's AI responded in his typical clipped British tones, unperturbed by the fact that people who were not them were suddenly in their base. "Magical incursions at multiple locations."

She grabbed her glasses and slipped them on. "Schematic to my display." An overlay of the vimana appeared with blue dots for the agents' current locations and red dots representing their unknown visitors. A *lot* of red dots, moving in discrete clusters of four. Diana had no trouble recognizing them as assault teams. She met Cara's eyes and said calmly, "Alfred, initiate scenario Zulu."

CHAPTER ELEVEN

Tony and Sloan had been assigned quarters near the center point of the facility, specifically in case one of the defense scenarios was invoked. Zulu was the most extreme, and Tony's heart pounded as he shoved his feet into a pair of boots and quickly tied the laces. He grabbed his glasses and slid them onto his face as he exited, finding Sloan already in the hallway. The other man asked, "Know anything?"

Tony shook his head. "Nothing. Got a lot of red dots, though."

"Better get geared up, then."

The team had been experimenting with quick deployment technology for some time. Kayleigh and Hank worked locally, consulting with Emerson, the big brain of the bunch, who participated by remote. Tony slapped a button on the wall, and the panel beside it rose to reveal an armored exoskeleton, the fruit of their labors. He stepped back into it, and once positioned to the satisfaction of the sensors inside, servos whined, and robot arms came to life.

Sections of armor descended to attach to the exoskeleton as it wrapped around him. He'd forgotten to take off his glasses, and a robot arm plucked them from his face right before the helmet went on. The suits weren't full combat models like the military or the AET might deploy in. They were custom prototypes, lighter than standard, and modified with primarily defensive armaments, a better fit for their needs in the vimana. *Or even for use in the field, the way we do things.*

As the final pieces latched together, his helmet display finished its boot-up process and showed him a two-hundred-and-seventy-degree view. A side window showed the feed from the camera on the back of his head that covered the rest of the surrounding space. He stepped forward, and the motors inside the suit handled its weight perfectly. Movement was only slightly clumsier than normal, not enough to cause significant problems.

The only things he lost in the exoskeleton were his ability to quick-draw and a touch of natural accuracy. The former wasn't necessary since a combination rifle and grenade launcher currently filled his hands. The red dot that appeared on his display at the partial press of either of the weapon's triggers handled the latter by showing where a given round would land. A pistol was present at the suit's thigh, and a plethora of other gadgets was within easy reach, attached to the exoskeleton.

Sloan stepped out of his cubby, identically armed and armored. "All good. These things rock. Where to, Stark?"

While they were all excellent combatants and tacticians, Sloan's expertise was more on the intelligence end of the spectrum, so Stark was the natural leader of the pair where fighting was concerned. Kayleigh's voice sounded over the comm, sounding a little breathless. "Primary doors fell as planned. Stark, Face, ready for me to funnel the scumbags to you?"

Tony replied, "Affirmative. Send in the clowns."

The tech chuckled. "Done. Be careful."

Diana's voice spoke next. "High probability these are from the US government. Nonlethal where possible. If you have to kill to save yourself, do, but evacuate instead if that's an option."

He slid the selector lever on his rifle over, telling the weapon to use the feed from the canister filled with crowd control ammunition. The munitions themselves were tiny, only about twice as big as a normal bullet, but they packed a punch disproportionate to their small size. When the first opposition squad appeared, he and Sloan launched simultaneously.

The mini-grenades flew down the hallway. He'd selected electricity rounds designed to short out the equipment the enemy would doubtless be carrying. When he realized they wore extremely high-tech-looking armor, he figured it probably wouldn't work. True to that expectation, the grenade landed, discharged, and utterly failed to stop or slow anyone.

Sloan's magazine had a web grenade loaded in the first position. It proved more successful, shooting strands of sticky adhesive across the lead enemy and onto the walls and floors. Tony launched his next round, also a web grenade, and ordered, "Fall back. Glam, they look like trouble. Make sure they don't get reinforcements for a minute or two."

The tech replied in the affirmative. Bullets flew, *clanging* off the interlocking armor plates that covered most of his torso and limbs. Normally he'd have Kevlar and his normal heavy ballistic cloth underneath, but the attack had come early enough in the morning that he wasn't in uniform and hadn't had time to get there.

All the agents slept in some clothes against the possibility of moving quickly, but that didn't include combat gear. *Or my gloves, or any of my other fun stuff.* He sent another grenade flying down the hallway, this one a flash-bang according to his display, knowing it would likely do nothing since their enemies wore full helmets and probably had the same sort of countermeasures they did.

He and Sloan stepped into small indentations in the walls, large enough to provide cover to shoot from. His finger reached for the rifle's trigger, then he grumbled and put it back on the one that activated the launcher. Three more grenades flew, only the single web attack having any effect. Even then, all it managed was to slow the enemy, who chopped at the strands with blades and shot at them with what sounded like shotguns. Tony shook his head. "We can't stay nonfatal and stop them. We can only delay them."

Diana replied, "Adequate. Hold them for as long as reasonable, then portal out."

Rath leapt down from the top bunk bed and grabbed his equipment. Max, his Borzoi companion, wasn't asleep below him, which was a problem. He shoved on the glasses he only used in the base and said, "Gwen. Locate Max." He strapped on his batons, wishing he'd also stored his knives and flight gear in his quarters. He ran out the door, and his personal AI, who had originally been there to help him fly but was now much more capable, illuminated a path on the floor.

She said, "Max is in the canteen."

He laughed. "Good. I was hungry anyway." He flew down the hallways, watching on his display to see where the enemies were and charting a route to avoid them. At one point, he had to cross their vision, and he did so in a tumbling blur, laughing again as bullets spattered nowhere near quickly enough to catch him. *Fast troll is fast.*

He found the dog and grabbed his head, hugging him. "Okay, Maxie. Bad guys around. We have to go." The Borzoi dipped his muzzle, whether understanding the words, tone, or just happy to see him, Rath had no idea. "Follow me. Gwen, locate Diana." They moved stealthily toward her location, careful to avoid engaging any of the enemies.

Eventually, though, it became impossible to evade contact. A pair of sentries held a position at an intersection they had to cross. He knelt to whisper in Max's ear. "You run through. Go fast, curve rather than straight. They probably won't shoot at a dog, and you'll be too fast, anyway." He pointed at the canine's eyes. "Do *not* get hurt."

The dog's muscles flexed under his hand, and Rath patted him as he drew his batons. "Go." His reasoning proved true as the Borzoi raced through the intersection, barking before he got there, which was both smart and something Rath should've thought of ahead of time. *Stupid. Be better.*

With their attention on his dog, neither of the guards reacted in time to avoid his attack. He dashed into the intersection and smashed them both in the legs with his batons, four strikes fast enough that his targets dropped to the floor before they realized what was going on. With their heads tipped back, he had access to flesh under their helmets, and he shoved his batons into the opening. They snapped as the stun function deployed, and both men's arms flopped to the sides.

He muttered, "Lucky there were only two," and headed for the Vault, the storage location for the artifacts they hadn't turned over to the government and the spot where the light on the schematic indicating Diana's presence pulsed softly.

CHAPTER TWELVE

Hank hit the deck running the moment the alarm went off. He held a vital role in all the scenarios that involved defending the base, which was getting to the armory and making sure it was defended and locked down. He raced through the hallways, guided by Alfred along a path that would allow him to stay away from enemy soldiers. The floor was cold on his toes, and he momentarily wished he'd paused to at least grab his boots. *Doesn't matter. There will be some in the armory.*

Keeping enemies out of the place where they kept their most important tech and magic—well, aside from the artifacts—was vital, and he'd honestly been honored Diana entrusted him with it. Of course, he had a backup. They all did. Anik joined him as he turned into the final corridor that led to their destination. The other man asked, "Any problems getting here?"

Hank shook his head. "None. The AI did its job."

They dashed inside and swung the heavy, oversized door closed. All the doors in the vimana were weird, not quite rectangular, and seemingly built for people far taller than them. Anik said, "We should probably throw the bolts."

Hank looked at the series of thick metal bars, eight in all, that would secure the portal at need. "No, let's wait. Alfred, give us eyes on all the approaches to this room, please." His glasses filled with small windows showing various corridors that were proximate to the armory. The AI would make the images flash if anyone entered the cameras' views.

Khan said, "Alfred, Zulu checklist, please." A list of tasks they had to complete to lock down the armory appeared. The agents kept their regular gear in standard lockers, and they wouldn't be able to do much about that stuff. Given the number of enemies flooding the base, they didn't have enough time to pack things up, even if they threw the bolts. Hank muttered, "Have to assume they came prepared, right?"

The special items, those were different. Whatever the team members thought was particularly important to them that didn't live in their quarters sat in boxes at one end of the room. The other agents had taken Khan and Hank to the places they wanted their stuff moved to, so they could open portals to those locations now. They pushed the containers through, hoping the destinations would be as secure as they were nine months ago when they'd set up this process.

When they finished, each man opened their special crate and grabbed the backpacks within, making sure they had their gear as well. Hank imagined that Khan had filled his with things that went boom. His pack held as many tools as weapons. *Custom tools, to be fair.*

He frowned as Kayleigh's voice came on the line. "The base's systems have detected that the enemies are carrying portable anti-magic emitters." The tech probably had advice to give, but that wasn't her role in the situation. Unlike most of the rest of the time, they were all following the rules to the letter.

Diana sounded like she was running. "Okay. Everybody, keep an eye on the enemy's progress. If they seem like they're going to get close to you, portal out regardless of whether you completed your tasks. Staying alive and free to fight another day is more important than anything here."

Hank thought, *not sure I agree with that, to be honest.* The base held a ton of information and a lot of tech they'd been working on that he'd hate to see fall into enemy hands. Still, it was neither his call nor his responsibility. Diana said, "We're fifteen seconds from the vault. Alfred, go into full lockdown in twenty seconds."

Rath's voice joined the channel, saying, "Thirty seconds. Need thirty."

Diana corrected, "Alfred, belay last. Thirty-five seconds to full lockdown."

More voices weighed in, and Hank took a moment to look at the feeds from all the cameras. No one was in view, which meant they could probably shoot the bolts now. *You never know.* "As soon as the base goes into lockdown, you and I throw the bars and get out of here. The boss is right. If we're free, we can help anyone who isn't."

Khan nodded. "Well, since you're my ride, I guess I have to agree with you."

Hank laughed. "Damn straight."

Kayleigh shouted, "You almost done in there?"

Deacon, sounding half-annoyed and half-remorseful, shouted back, "You know, setting a year of one's work up to self-destruct isn't really a good time. Cut me some slack, woman."

She sighed and shook her head. Her hands were busily shoving devices, supplies, and tools into two large duffel bags, each of which would be a challenge for her to carry. Fortunately, all they had to do was throw them through a portal. "I'm sure you have copies of everything on the magical dark web, or whatever you call it."

He laughed, but it held no humor. "Actually, no, that would be... Unsafe. What I have are hard drives and the hope that nothing gets corrupted on them now that they're the only extant copy of my life's work."

"Drama Queen." Despite her words, she acutely felt the same pain as she decided what to take with her and what to abandon. She prioritized fabrication materials rather than repair supplies since the next phase of Zulu would leave her on her own for a while. *Hopefully not too long.*

She'd been part of developing the scenario. All of them had. Diana had described the various threats they'd potentially face, and the team had brainstormed options together.

After they developed them, they rehearsed the ones that

seemed most promising and finally set twenty-six of them in stone, Alpha through Zulu. Of those that involved base defense, the one the boss had selected was the most extreme. For Diana to call for it indicated she must have some extra knowledge about what might be coming against them. *Probably from the information we decoded. It's a good thing Deacon is so amazing at his work.*

A small bell sounded as Alfred activated full lockdown on the base. Heavy doors descended to seal off corridors at twelve-foot intervals, which would significantly impede the attackers' movement through the building. The area outside the labs had its own main door, and even with the best cutting gear, it would take them a while to get through it.

Deacon bustled into the room, shrugging a backpack onto his shoulders. "Okay, I'm good. How can I help?"

"I thought two bags would be enough, but three would be better. Maybe four. Grab some, will you? The lockdown should give us plenty of time to fill them up."

He complied, but she lost track of him as a camera feed in her glasses drew her attention. It showed a differently suited person moving forward at a calm pace. His body armor seemed more advanced than those around him, and instead of carrying a weapon, he had a large case with him. He set it down and opened it, revealing several strange-looking objects of varying shapes.

She frowned, not understanding what she was seeing but feeling like it wasn't good. "Alfred, feed this to the boss." She activated a channel directly to Diana and said, "We've got something weird here."

Diana replied, "I see it. Any guesses?"

Kayleigh shook her head. "No, although those things look a lot like some of the vimana's strange metal."

"Yeah, I was thinking the same thing."

The person on the screen placed one of the objects against the wall next to a lowered door, and it immediately slid open. Then, to her horror, the cameras in her display showed the defensive barricades opening up throughout the facility.

Diana said, "Shit," then her voice came over the channel that fed everyone. "They have access to the vimana's control systems. Throw physical latches immediately and get the hell out. Right damn now."

Kayleigh turned to Deacon and growled, with a grumbled curse. "Figures. Okay, one and a half bags will have to do. Open the portal."

He obeyed, and she saw the small apartment she'd rented through a series of cutouts and false names on the opposite side. It looked appropriately disused, as she hadn't been there in a month or so and dust accumulated with no apparent cause.

She pushed one bag through and slung the other over her shoulder. She crossed the threshold, then turned to face Deacon. "You know, we could break the rules here. You could come with me."

He shook his head. "No, they're there for a reason. Even you need to follow these."

She tried to ignore the sensation of her heart sinking into her stomach. "Be careful, Deke."

He gave her a confident grin. "You know it, Kitana. See you online."

The portal closed, leaving Kayleigh truly alone for the

first time in more than a year. She sat on the edge of the bed and fought back the tears that wanted to come.

After portaling his girlfriend away, Deacon ran into his workspace. The self-destruct required both virtual commands and physical switches. He'd already accomplished the former, but he hadn't been able to bring himself to do the latter, somehow hoping things would work out so he didn't need to. Clearly, though, that was no longer a possibility.

He'd worked with Anik to lace the server racks with explosives, a particular setup that wouldn't be affected by heat, or static, or anything. He opened the first protective panel on the right wall and hit the button underneath, then crossed to the left wall and repeated the process with the trigger there.

In several locations, liquids formerly kept separate started to mix, creating an explosive compound that flowed through transparent tubes wrapped along the frames of the server racks. He ran from the room, closing the heavy door five seconds before the system added the catalyst. Sounds of many moderate explosions came through the closed barrier, signaling the destruction of his prized gear.

He growled, "I'm going to make it my life's work, dedicating all my free time to it, to getting revenge on the people who made me do that. Count on it. I declare a vendetta."

With one last look back, he opened the portal to his safe house and strode through.

———

Diana threw the heavy bolts that protected the inward swinging door of the vault. Once they'd discovered that certain rooms had doors that didn't lift into the ceiling, those had become locations for important things like the vault, the armory, and their gathering place for several other scenarios. Rath, who had arrived with Max on his heels mere seconds before, asked, "Do we know who they are?"

She replied, "I have a pretty good guess. That's a problem for another day. Start filling bags."

Over the next five minutes, a six-foot-tall Rath managed to fill two duffels while Diana and Cara unlocked the safes holding the most valuable items. Their packing time ended as Alfred warned, "Enemies approaching the vault." She focused her eyes on the camera windows in her glasses and saw that indeed, they *were* getting close, and they carried heavy tools, plus explosives. Given what they'd accomplished so far, she couldn't trust that their defenses would hold for long. "Guess we're done here."

Cara shook her head sadly. "You know, I really like this place. There was something cool about the purity of living the job. Haven't felt that since early days in the Army."

She managed a smile. "I get that. I agree. It was pretty idyllic. That alone should have told us it was too good to be true."

Rath, now returned to his three-foot form, laughed. "It's a new adventure. Look forward, not back."

Diana sighed at the troll's giddiness. "How about you take him with you, Cara?"

The other woman had already opened a portal but paused before stepping through to reply, "Oh, hell no. I'll watch the dog, though."

Rath patted Max and said, "No chance, no way, no. We're a package deal."

The other woman grinned at them, seeming more emotional than usual. "Be careful. Be well. See you soon." Then she stepped through and was gone.

Diana looked down at her magical life partner. "You ready, buddy?" He nodded. "Alfred, anyone on our side left but us?"

The AI replied, "Negative."

Then she gave the command she'd hoped never to have to give. "Okay, Alfred, Clean Slate. Execute."

The AI's neutral tone answered, "Confirmation code?"

Diana intoned the poorly rearranged words of the philosopher Camus. "I believe in nothing, and everything is absurd."

"Acknowledged." The instruction would release a computer worm Deacon had developed into all the base's connected systems. It would go through everything they'd created before coming to Antarctica and everything they'd added since getting here, months and months before. Codes, records, data from their daily calendars to remote piloting functions for their vehicles. *All of it, gone. Poof.*

Diana shook herself out of her haze. "All right, Rath. New adventure it is."

CHAPTER THIRTEEN

Bryant's watch woke him from a sound sleep, the alarm a pattern he didn't recognize. He sat up and pulled his glasses on, eyes widening at the sight of the red dots on the base schematic. He jumped out of bed and gave the commands to join the comm channels, listening in as Diana initiated scenario Zulu.

He released a guttural snarl of frustration as he ran for his closet. *Didn't take the bastards much time to move. Our information came a beat too late. I wonder if Finley is compromised.*

He didn't entertain any suspicion that the senator would actively work against him. They'd been allies too long for that. However, it was entirely possible the man was being fed misinformation or denied access to things he should have the ability to see. "Emma, building surveillance, please."

A lush British accent approximating the voice of Emma Peel from the old *Avengers* television show replied, "Acknowledged," and the display in his glasses changed.

The left side showed feeds from several tiny cameras he'd positioned throughout the structure. The right provided images from the building's security systems.

He lived on one of the middle floors of a thirty-story apartment tower, figuring that assured him the greatest possible anonymity and the most protection. He couldn't wall himself in or hide in the suburbs, given his role as a pseudo-politician. *Really, I guess what I am is a very focused lobbyist working for all the ARES bureaus.*

He finished pulling on his suit, having slid a low-profile bulletproof vest on under his shirt and laced up his heavy-duty boots. They were steel-toed and heeled, in case he needed to kick someone, and held a knife and a holster, respectively. He opened the large gun safe at the rear of the room, the first turn of the wheel coinciding with the appearance of a tactical team on one of his cameras.

By the time he had the container open, he'd spotted several more teams moving in from both the lobby and the roof toward his floor. "Emma, lock down the elevators."

She replied, "Done, Bryant."

He had multiple countermeasures in place to activate in his defense, but that was the easiest one. The people coming up from below wouldn't enjoy the entrapment, nor would they appreciate having to walk up the many flights of stairs to get to him. He snapped on his equipment belt, which looked normal from the front but had several useful devices that hid under his suit coat.

His 10mm Glock 40 pistol went into a holster at his lower back, and he stuffed his Sig Sauer P238 pistol into his boot. Finally, he grabbed a pair of heavy-duty black Tasers and headed for the door.

The camera showed the hallway outside his apartment was clean, so he exited quietly and headed toward the stairs going up. Logic suggested there would be fewer enemies in that direction. He'd considered simply portaling out, strictly following the rules of the scenario, but he was furious at his lack of forewarning.

He didn't blame himself entirely for the situation in the vimana. Still, he felt that if he'd been better at navigating the weird political currents that always swirled around Washington, he might've been able to give them more time to prepare. *Now I'm going to find someone who will tell me exactly what the hell is going on, so I'm more on the ball if something like this is ever in the works again.*

He ascended several flights, then heard a tactical team advancing from above. He stepped out into the empty hallway ahead of their arrival. His camera showed plain-clothes agents knocking on doors on his floor, apparently asking his neighbors about him. *They really put on a full-court press here. I wonder if they'll go to the other levels?*

His initial plan had been to take down one of the four-person units and interrogate whoever was still conscious at the end of it, but he liked these odds better. He watched from his cameras as a tactical team broke into his apartment. When they didn't find him there, new orders went out because the agents questioning his neighbors moved directly to the stairwells. The fact that tactical teams went with them put a crimp in his revised plan to capture one of the non-armored opposition.

Damn, damn, damn. Okay. Time to get out of here. He summoned his magic to create a portal and blinked in surprise when it failed to materialize. His brain added two and two together, remembered the armored troops had been wearing backpacks and further recalled Kayleigh's warning about anti-magic emitters in the base. *Oh, you want to do it the hard way, then? Okay, I'm game.*

If he were running the op, he'd have those on every floor. He would also plant surveillance and traps in case the quarry evaded the perimeter. *Interesting that they brought anti-magic for me. Not everyone knows I'm a magical.*

He wore polished wooden rings on his fingers that served as his wands, one that had been with him forever and another more recent creation that he was still in the process of fully bonding with. Their carvings were different enough that no one should immediately assume they were a matched set, only that he liked elegant wooden rings.

He descended quietly to the floor above his, which held a dispersed tactical team and an agent. He walked boldly through the door from the stairwell, approaching the single guard watching the hallway. Each floor had four corridors arranged in a rectangle, so the four-person team had logically deployed one to each. The guard's armor meant that any shot from a distance with the Taser probably wouldn't hit anywhere it could do any damage, and he didn't want to start gunfighting quite yet if he could help it.

The man lifted his rifle and shouted for Bryant to stop, but he shook his head and put a hand to his ear, then threw the device he'd palmed before leaving the stairwell. A small gas grenade bounced once, then went off at the man's feet. He'd gambled that the helmet wouldn't also be a gas mask, and the way his opponent collapsed confirmed the notion.

He peeled off the other man's helmet and took his

headset, pressing the earpiece against his head to listen. No alarm sounded, and the chatter was all tactical, offering nothing useful.

He sighed and dropped the communication gear on the guard's body. Then he dragged the fallen man to the stairwell, stripped him out of his armor, and put it on over his suit. Zip ties would keep his foe from moving when he woke up, and the stairs had good soundproofing.

He descended the staircase into the lobby and casually exited the building. Outside, they'd parked a command post trailer along the curb and positioned several police department cars for backup and to block the street. He shook his head at the idea that they'd gone through all that effort to catch him and angled toward the command trailer. He pounded on the door, and when someone opened it from within, he pushed his way inside and latched it again behind him.

The long vehicle held two guards, four technicians, and a guy in a suit giving orders. He threw a stun grenade at the group clustered around the instrument panel, and its detonation wreathed the techs and their boss in electricity. It was enough to daze them, which would give him all the time he needed. He charged the nearest guard, ramming his knee up between the man's legs and slamming an armored elbow into his helmet. He repeated the strike three times, and finally, the man went down.

Bryant spun toward the other guard, who was at the far end of the trailer. His opponent had gotten his gun out of its holster. Bryant grabbed another disc from the back of his belt and hurled it across the space between them. This one was an Emerson special, a powerful magnet that activated when it struck.

It hit the gun, latched on, and yanked the weapon and the arm that refused to release it toward the side of the truck. During the ensuing confusion, Bryant pushed his way through the techs and kicked the guard in the leg, forcing him down to a knee, then delivered several blows to his head from above.

The man collapsed, and Bryant turned and tased two technicians, the sensory overload rendering them instantly unconscious. He ejected the cartridges, quickly replaced them, and took out the other pair before they were fully functional again.

Calls were coming over the speakers in the truck, asking questions that no one except the guy in the suit would be able to answer. Bryant grabbed the boss and slapped him, then yanked off his helmet. The other man's eyes widened, and he nodded. "Yeah. It's me. Here's the thing. Going after my team was a bad move. Tell me who's in charge, and you get to live through this."

The other man shook his head, and Bryant slapped him a second time with enough force to open his lip and redden his face. "Try again. Seriously. There's no reason for you to die because you're too stupid at this critical moment to give me the information I'm going to find out anyway."

Without releasing his captive, he reached under his pant leg, pulled out the hidden knife, and pushed it up under the man's chin. "My options are diminishing second by second. I need to get out of here before you folks force me to kill a lot of people. Last chance to get to go home tonight."

The man swallowed and tried to stretch his throat away from the blade's point. "Serrano. It's his op. Not sure why. Said you and your people are traitors."

Bryant smashed an elbow into the man's face before fully realizing he intended to do it, then rammed his helmet back on and stomped out of the trailer, shoving the door closed behind him. *Traitor? We'll see who's a traitor and who's not.*

No one tried to stop the uniformed man striding with a purpose toward the perimeter. He dropped the anti-magic emitter backpack as soon as he turned the corner, then continued walking, testing his magic with small things every few seconds. When it finally returned, he opened a portal and crossed the threshold to safety.

CHAPTER FOURTEEN

Kevin Serrano replaced his pistol in its shoulder holster and zipped up the leather jacket designed to conceal it with a nod to the security guards at the checkpoint. He had special dispensation to carry his weapon anywhere he went, short of the White House. *Big responsibilities, big privileges. I'll need every one of them to get this job done.*

Sometimes when he visited the Senate building, he played the game, wore the suit, left the gun at home, generally tried to fit in. Today, the day after things had finally gotten rolling, he wasn't interested in pretending to be anyone other than who he was. His close-cropped black hair was shorter than he'd worn it in the Special Forces, a sacrifice to his time being too valuable to spend it worrying about his looks.

After his eight trips around the sun on active duty, he'd gone military intelligence, then CIA. Twenty years out of high school, he had a job he wouldn't have dreamed of being able to possess back at the start of his career. *That's why I'm not going to let anything fuck it up.*

He waved away a volunteer guide that served tourists in the building. He knew where he was going. When he arrived at the conference room, both senators from Nevada were present. Carter Richardson, the Republican, and Stella Borowski, the Democrat.

He looked like his name, tall, thin, blonde, totally country club. She was also tall, but the similarity ended there since she had dark hair, dark eyes, and a sense of seriousness that the other lacked.

He'd been surprised to find these two leading the charge against Sheen and Bates, but they'd found common ground on this particular issue. *Maybe because of all the chaos in Magic City lately. They don't want to see it spill over to Vegas and slay the golden goose.* He put a smile on his face to hide his thoughts. "Senators. We ready?"

They nodded, and he set a small device, a little larger than a cell phone, on the large conference table. He whispered the command to activate his comm, then said, "Tash, got me?"

A female voice replied, "Affirmative."

"Well, come on then. Quit wasting time." He poked his second-in-command whenever the opportunity presented itself since most of the time, she was flawlessly capable.

A portal opened on the table, and a witch stepped through. She didn't look like a witch, or at least not the stereotype of one. Shortish spiky blonde hair crowned her head, and black tactical pants, a black t-shirt, and a short sleeve button down on top of it covered her body. Her face held more than a little makeup, applied to make it noticeable. She jumped down, and he smiled at the senators.

Richardson said, fairly calmly, given what he'd just witnessed, "You're not supposed to be able to portal in here. Anti-magic emitters and whatnot." His voice was deeper than expected.

Kevin nodded. "We have the technology. That little beauty creates a space where anti-magic emitters are blocked. It also provides a homing beacon." The witch held up a similar-looking device, and he continued, "Which can be received by that one. They only talk to each other. The signal can't be tapped under any circumstances or even detected until one of the devices is activated."

Borowski said, "That seems dangerous."

"It is. This whole thing is, and that's why you asked me to be here. Now, make sure those doors are locked, please. I'm going to use another, so we can take a look at the traitors' base. This one will stay here to provide a way back, and we don't want anyone stumbling over it."

Richardson nodded. "I'll send for my aide to guard the room from outside, with instructions that we're not to be bothered."

After a delay for the senators to wrap up things that needed wrapping up, they crossed the distance from Washington, D.C. to Antarctica in a single step. The portal had opened into the hallway outside the armory, and he and Tash escorted the politicians into the equipment-filled space. Richardson said, "Holy cow. Look at all the stuff."

Kevin laughed. "Yeah. They were well-funded, and they put the funding to good use."

TR CAMERON

Borowski shook her head. "They couldn't have had enough cash for all this stuff."

He shrugged, although he tended to agree with her. "No evidence exists to prove they were skimming. Apparently, they managed some very effective spending. Plus, of course, they might've taken some of the gear dropped by people on the other side."

Richardson said, "It's like Christmas for your group, yes? Can you take all this equipment for yourselves?"

Tash nodded, familiar enough with his responses to such questions to answer. "We, too, are perennially underfunded." *Lie. We're not. But it wouldn't be good for you two to know that. You might think of reducing our funding, which would never do.*

Kevin said, "Getting this gear was the most successful part of the mission."

The witch snorted. "You mean the *only* fully successful part."

"More accurate, less tactful."

She grinned. "That's me in a nutshell."

They reached the tech area, and both senators frowned at the destruction in the space to the right. Richardson said, "Let me guess. Main computers?"

Kevin nodded. "First pitch, right out of the park. They doubled up the damage to them, just to be sure. First, a worm chewed through all the data. Then they physically blew up the servers.

"We only know about the worm because a couple of fragments survived, but they're useless. In fact, worse than useless because as soon as we started looking at them, the damn worm tried to infiltrate our systems."

Borowski asked, "Is that normal?"

Kevin shook his head. "No. It's sophisticated programming. More than we thought they had. Likely imbued with magic."

Richardson gestured at the rest of the space. "This is the tech area? Gadget making and stuff?"

"Yep. They didn't clean it out quite as well, but it held no surprises. We already knew they were working on the things left behind in here from reports or surveillance."

Borowski turned to him and said, "Maybe this is a good time for you to explain how you got so much information on them. This is probably the most secure location we'll ever have."

He chuckled. "Actually, for all we know, they could still have surveillance going here, so it may not be all that safe. Still, that might work to our benefit because any signal that leaves this place is something we can track and hopefully use to find them. Anyway, we used a mix of electronic surveillance, human intelligence, and a few clever new spy gadgets that are bleeding edge." He gestured for them to start walking again and led them out of the room.

"One of our people was here for a tour, all aboveboard and planned, and they deposited a couple of super-miniature devices. They're only capable of blasting back small amounts of data, and only when conditions are perfect, but it was enough to let us know they weren't following the rules we'd agreed upon at the beginning." They took a turn toward the artifact vault.

Richardson asked, "Specifically, where did they misstep? Surely you can share that now."

When he'd informed the senators about the operation,

he'd claimed that all the evidence was under a judge's seal. That hadn't been even remotely true, but it was enough to give him reasonable deniability. Plus, he knew people who could be convinced or coerced to support the lie at need. "I'll show you, just ahead."

They walked the rest of the way to the vault in silence. Well, more accurately, Kevin and Tash remained quiet. The politicians babbled between themselves, remarking on the strange metal, the odd shapes of the place, and the weird symbols that showed up now and again.

He'd researched the vimana inside and out before committing to the operation, so none of it was new to him. Plus, except for his trip back to Washington to get the senators, he'd been in the facility since they'd taken it, gathering data and checking things out. Going through people's quarters had initially made him a little uncomfortable until he remembered that they'd turned against the government. After that, he felt fine rooting through their stuff.

They entered the vault, and he gestured at the shelves and safes. "According to their paperwork, they were turning over all the artifacts they found during their missions, save a couple. However, those numbers didn't seem right. That's what got us on their track in the first place."

Richardson asked, "How many?"

"We estimate they kept back half, roughly. We're fairly confident that in that half were some of the most powerful items."

Borowski touched one of the transparent boxes stacked on the shelves with a finger as if expecting the falcon-shaped metal and stone object inside it to leap out at her. "How can you be sure?"

"We know they faced certain extremely powerful magical artifacts in the field. We know they won those battles, and we further know they didn't turn those items over. So, unless they vanished or Sheen abandoned them at the scene, it stands to reason that they kept them. Probably for personal use."

The senator turned from inspecting the box and asked, "Aren't those things infectious, somehow?"

Tash laughed. "By infectious, do you mean they crawl inside your flesh, bond with you whether you want them to or not, and do their best to manipulate your mind into doing things that civilized folks generally wouldn't do? If so, then the answer is yes."

Richardson shook his head. "Why did we give them that much latitude in the first place?"

Kevin replied, "I couldn't say. I probably would've wound up making the same decision. Sheen had made a name for herself, Bates's work was exemplary in all respects, and gathering the artifacts was a job that needed doing. Given the remoteness of this location, storing them here was perfectly logical. The only error was not maintaining more oversight."

Richardson snapped, "So it's Bates's fault."

"It's *all* our faults, Senator. We offered trust in a time when trust is too valuable a gift to give. We should've had eyes on them constantly, including someone here at the base."

Borowski asked, "What's the next step?" The tone of

interest, maybe wonder, had left her voice, which was now utterly businesslike.

Tash replied, "We find them and bring them to justice, one way or the other."

"You know I'm not in favor of shoot on sight operations. Neither of us is."

Kevin nodded. "As they've done nothing overt to attack the government, we're hoping theft is as far as they were willing to go. So, we'll give them a chance to surrender whenever we can."

Richardson observed, "Guess we can't ask for more than that."

"Not against these people. Every one of them is too skilled, too powerful. We'll do what we can to keep the peace, but if it's them or us, they're going down."

CHAPTER FIFTEEN

Diana pulled the bedroom curtain slightly aside and looked out the window, shivering as frigid air snuck through the space between the frame and the wall. "When I decided our bolt hole should be on Cape Cod, I'd forgotten how wicked the winters are here."

Rath, sitting on the bed behind her, laughed. "That's okay. Max likes the cold." The dog barked from his position on the floor as if to agree with the troll.

Diana let the curtain fall and turned to her companion. "Well, you're going to be the one taking him for walks."

He giggled. "Neighbors might notice. Troll walking a dog. Not something you see every day."

She sighed. "Yeah, you're not wrong. Let's head downstairs."

The house was small, originally someone's vacation home, and more recently repurposed as a rental. It had two bedrooms, one bathroom, a kitchen, and a combination living and dining room. Reserving it for the winter was a reasonably priced solution to needing a spot to lie low.

No paper trail connected her to the location. Lisa's parents had stayed there once, years before, and Diana had visited, which had put the place on her radar. The arrangement was through a fictitious name and a fictitious company, and she trusted Deacon's handiwork completely.

They'd spent the hours since arriving lying low, keeping quiet, and watching out the windows to see if any strange activity was happening nearby. None manifested. Not only no suspicious activity but no activity at all. A blanket of snow covered the ground from a storm a couple of days before, and the snowplows apparently didn't bother to come down this far. She'd have to make up some story about how they got to the place to avoid revealing who they were if questioned. It didn't worry her. She'd go out when it was dark and use magic to clear a path they might've used to get the house.

Now, it was time to get things organized since they might be staying for a while. She went into the kitchen and opened the cupboards, finding them stocked as she'd requested. They held many canned foods, some staples like rice and beans, and some dehydrated milk.

A chest freezer in the mudroom contained an abundance of prepackaged meals, as well as a bunch of pizza squares because her companion was pretty partial to them. *Like, obsessed.* She threw a couple of dinners in the microwave, then spent the minutes while they cooked further acquainting herself with the kitchen.

When they were ready, she sat down at the table and kicked a chair out for Rath. Max barked from beside her leg, and she frowned down at him. "You wait, mister.

There's food for you, too. You're as bad as he is." She gestured with her chin at the figure on the opposite side.

Rath grinned. "Growing troll needs food badly."

She chuckled. "Maybe you should eat at your smallest size. Then it wouldn't cost so much to feed you."

"Doesn't work that way. When I got bigger, I'd need more. Why are you trying to starve me?"

Diana knew that. They discussed it all before. They were only babbling. It felt good to babble, given what they'd been through. Their world had come crashing down around them, and nothing was the same as it had been only ten hours before. She wasn't sure of the reasons behind the attack on the vimana, and the Zulu protocol wouldn't let her contact anyone to find out. But eventually, she *would* find out, and when she did, trouble was going to pay those responsible a visit.

She checked her watch and saw that they had a little over an hour and forty-five minutes until it would be exactly half a day since she'd invoked scenario Zulu. That was an important time point, and they needed to be ready. Until then, they had no specific requirements. She mentioned the timeframe to Rath, and the troll replied, "We should go for a walk and check out the neighborhood. See who's around, see what's nearby. Maybe meet the neighbors."

It was an appealing idea but not a practical one. "We're going to need to lie low for a few days. Chances are good that whoever attacked the base will be looking for us, and they pretty well know that you and I are a team. Even if we use illusion to hide, two new people showing up are bound to generate suspicion. Sure, most of it would be friendly community gossip stuff, but you never know. Word could get out. We should wait a bit."

Rath nodded, looking thoughtful. "That's pretty thin, worry-wise."

She laughed. "The thinnest, but we need to be ultra-careful right now. Let's go down to the basement and grab our gear."

Diana hadn't retrieved the equipment she'd transported to the house some months before yet. She'd feared the potential for discovery and surveillance and wanted to be ready to run at an instant's notice, not trapped in the basement. Now, though, she felt like that probably wasn't likely, that if it were going to happen, it already would have. She pulled the cord on an old bare bulb in a socket as they walked down the stairs, then did the same again with another when they made it to the bottom.

The basement was freezing, with cold concrete walls radiating the winter chill through the room. A heavy old wardrobe stood in one corner, a mammoth piece of furniture that was easily four hundred pounds empty. It was full of stuff, the collected debris of many years including paint cans, tools, screws and nails, odds and ends. She used her magic to levitate the behemoth, pushed it to the side with muscle power, then set it gently back down a few feet away.

A wooden panel painted to look like the floor covered a small compartment underneath where the wardrobe had been. Diana removed the cover, reached in, and pulled out a duffel bag. Sliding the first across to Rath, she extracted a second.

She replaced the cover and returned to the wardrobe to

its original spot in a reverse of the earlier process, ensuring there would be no scrapes or scuffs to suggest anything unusual existed in the basement. She cursed softly and rubbed her hands together. "Okay, upstairs, you two. *Damn,* it's cold."

Max and Rath bounded up the stairs ahead of her, and she carried the duffels, one hanging from her left hand, the other slung on her back like a backpack. It was entirely unlikely anyone would find them in this place and unlikelier still that an attack would come this quickly even if their enemies had found them. Still, she wasn't about to compromise both of her hands at the same time if any other option existed.

She closed the door to the basement, sealing the cold inside, and set the duffel bags on chairs next to the dining room table. Rath climbed up on one of the seats, sitting on the back of it precariously so he'd have a good view of the table. He observed, "It's like my birthday."

Diana laughed. "Yeah, a birthday filled with used gifts." She unzipped the bag and started pulling out the troll's stuff. At the top was an equipment belt with two sheathed batons. "Don't need these, since you managed to bring your latest ones. Nice job on that." She set them aside.

The troll nodded. "Got lucky." The next item was the previous version of his flight gear, a harness with a large rectangular compartment on the back that held the wings. A pair of goggles went with it. She wasn't sure the glasses Rath had worn during their escape would interface with it since they were newer, so it was fortunate they were included. He asked, "Will the AI still work without the base linkup?"

It was a great question. While the programs were probably independent enough to work in the field without any other connection, they depended on the main computer for updates and such. Because Deacon and Kayleigh constantly upgraded their gear, it was unclear how many steps back this set's version of Gwen was, compared to the one he'd worked with recently. "I know they can function autonomously, but they might not have full functionality. I'm sure you'll have all the necessary flight controls, though."

He nodded, unable to conceal a grin. "Could need to experiment."

She laughed. "No, you are not jumping off high things here and sailing over the frozen ocean. We'll keep the wings, and if we can figure out a way for you to test them without being noticed, we will. I consider them a backup plan at the moment." A small snort escaped her. "That's *all* we need, some tabloid running headlines about the flying troll spotted on Cape Cod."

He giggled. "I'd be famous."

"You'd be dead, and me shortly after, since it would give away our location. As far as I know, you're the only troll with wings."

He nodded. "I'm special."

Diana laughed. "In more ways than one, buddy." The rest of his bag contained other older versions of his gear, including a vest with throwing knives that looked a little worn on the straps, a harness for Max that would allow Rath to ride him if appropriately configured, and boots. The boots weren't old, but here in the snow, he'd need some heavy footwear. They would shred if he grew, but that was preferable to having him lose toes to frostbite. *Assuming trolls can get frostbite. I don't see why they couldn't. I wonder if ice trolls are a thing.* She laughed internally. *Maybe they hang out with the abominable snowman.*

Out loud, she said, "We'll keep the gear with us on whatever floor we're spending the most time on. So, during the day down here, at night up in the bedroom."

He nodded. "Should've slept in full outfits."

Diana chuckled. "Yeah, right? If only." Shook her head. She had Fury because Hank had thrown it through from the armory, where she'd stupidly left it after her training session the night before the attack. *That was only yesterday. Damn.* She hoped everyone else had their most important gear as well. But they generally went unarmed in the vimana, so she didn't have her favorite pistol or even her regular backup pistol.

Her bag contained a sheathed katana she set aside, three pairs of worn tactical clothes and a pair of boots, and two gun cases. She opened the first and found her old Glock. She popped the magazine, noting that it was loaded with anti-magic bullets, and slid it home.

The case held another magazine full of the specialty rounds and a cleaning kit nestled in the foam cut-outs along the top. It was a gun she'd used in the past, so she was fairly confident it would be sound and the sights properly aligned. She would still clean it thoroughly before she trusted it not to blow up in her hand.

The other gun case revealed a Ruger LCP II, her previous backup weapon. It only had six shots but fit neatly in a boot holster and carried anti-magic rounds as well. Several times in the recent past, she'd been forced to go without her backup pistol because the new model was a little too bulky for some outfits. She'd thought fondly of this one in those moments and was frankly glad to see it again.

In addition to the holster on her right boot, the left held a narrow knife tucked into the back. They also had steel toes and heels to make her kicks more impactful. *Heh. Impact.* Her equipment belt had its battery attached, and an old pair of stun gloves was the last thing in the bag. They took more power to deliver less shock than her usual ones, but they'd still give her a useful edge. "This stuff is enough to keep us reasonably safe for the moment, but it's not nearly adequate for what lies ahead. We'll need more gear."

Rath nodded seriously. "Visit Nylotte?"

Diana shook her head. "Not right away. They'll *definitely* be watching her. No, she and I have a protocol for when we're out of contact, and we'll have to wait for that to activate. It takes a few days of non-communication. In the meantime, though, we might need to hit up one of the stashes."

Rath clapped. "Excellent. Shopping."

Diana laughed. "Yeah, that. But for at least the next twenty-four to thirty-six hours, we're not leaving this house except to take Max into the back yard." The troll looked a little sad at her words but brightened as she said, "On the plus side, we have a DVD player, a ton of movies, and pizza, popcorn, and other snacks in the cupboard. Movie marathon?"

Rath leapt into a somersault off the chair, landing and running toward the television. Movie nights were something they used to do often in their first days together, and the troll loved it. "Okay. I pick the films."

She groaned. "It's going to be all Stallone, isn't it?"

He slid to a stop and turned, pointing back at her. "I'll be the judge of that. I am the law."

CHAPTER SIXTEEN

Deacon had arrived at his hideaway spot and immediately gone on alert. Nothing was *obviously* out of place in the basement apartment, and he hadn't lived in the small town for quite a long time, making it reasonable to think it might not show up in an initial search of his history. The space was reasonably clean, with no sign that anyone had been inside or disturbed it.

Maybe that's the problem. Mrs. Carter, upstairs, wouldn't have come down here on her own. So why is it so neat? Just lucky? Do things not get as dusty as I think they do?

He spent five minutes walking through the rooms, looking for evidence to push him to one side of the question or the other before deciding something was wrong. Someone had to have been inside and tried to clean up the signs of their presence. *Which means they might be watching me right now or even have a capture team on the way.*

He had no idea how they might've located this place unless they very successfully dug into his background going back to his college days. That would only have given them the town, nothing more.

How doesn't matter. Only that they did. Probably. Or I'm paranoid. He opened a portal and stepped through it, emerging in the parking lot of a large shopping mall a hundred miles away. It was another town he'd lived in, but his residence had been on the far other side of it.

He entered the mall and walked for an hour, doing the surveillance checks the agents had taught him. When no sign of watchers appeared, he vectored into the taco restaurant at one end and ordered some food, paying in cash.

Deacon chose a table at the back where he could watch the door and kept his eyes peeled. After that turned up nothing, it was *another* hour spent wandering the mall, popping into shops that looked interesting to him, before he was confident enough that he didn't have a tail to take the next step. Finally, he went into the restroom of one of the anchor department stores, opened a portal, and stepped through to Kayleigh's safe house.

He managed to duck an instant before the baseball bat would've glanced off his head. She'd probably angled the blow away anyway, but it still might have caught him. He laughed at the expression on her face, which was somewhere in the middle of happy and furious. "Chill, slacker, it's only me."

She growled, "Don't do that, you jerk," dropped the bat, and wrapped him in a hug. He returned it gratefully, some of the tension of the past couple of hours leaving him.

Deacon asked, "Are you okay?"

Kayleigh took a step back and nodded, deftly brushing

a hand across her face in a gesture that could have just as easily been moving her hair away as wiping tears. He guessed it was a bit of the latter if she felt anything akin to the relief he felt. "Fine. No sign of surveillance. Why are you here?"

He frowned. "Got a negative vibe at my place. Hopped over to the mall to make sure no one was watching me, then came here."

"I have bad news."

"The others?"

She shook her head and quickly replied, "No, we're still a few hours away from check-in. Nothing from them yet. But, well, it's easier to show you."

He followed her into the office and saw what she meant. A window had broken, and snow had entered the room. Specifically, the snow had covered both of their computers, which, while loaded only with innocuous programs, were both high-powered models intended for use in this exact situation. "Bloody hell."

Kayleigh nodded. "Yeah, that's more or less what I said. Stupid happenstance."

Deacon shrugged, initial annoyance transforming into problem-solving mode. "Stuff happens, even to the good guys like us. It's no biggie." He checked his watch. "We probably have time to hit our stash and a big box store."

"Think it's safe?"

"I'd guess that aside from Diana and Rath, they won't look for any couples. While you do bear a slight resemblance to the troll, given your diminutive height, I look nothing like the boss."

She kicked him in the shin. "Don't push it, mister, or

you're sleeping in the snow room. Without a blanket. In the nude."

He laughed. "We'll probably need to hit a grocery store for some supplies, too. I sense a lot of calorie-burning computer work in my future."

"Okay. Let's do it."

The garage held a motorcycle and a couple of helmets, plus a can full of gas. They fueled it and headed out, the bike fishtailing a little as they swerved onto the street through a patch of snow. He asked, "Are you sure you know how to drive this thing?"

Kayleigh replied, "Shut it. I'm an expert."

He laughed. "That's what you said about the first version of the web grenade."

He could hear the scowl in her voice. "That was a defect in the canister."

"Uh-huh, sure it was." The fact that she'd had to spend hours cleaning up the mess ensured that particular incident remained a sore memory for the tech. He changed the subject. "Are we confident the stash is okay?"

Her helmet bobbed in a nod. "I dropped in on the nearby cameras a week or so ago. Through a series of cutouts, of course. No change."

He shook his head. "Only you could convince me to do something as goofy as putting our vital gear in a bus station locker. It's so stereotypical. Like we're in an eighties spy movie."

She laughed. Their helmets had microphones and earpieces physically connected through a cable, which allowed them to talk without fear of having their transmissions intercepted. "You're jealous you didn't think of it first."

When they got to the bus station, they went in together and stopped to buy some coffee from the snack bar, trying to look the part of travelers heading out. The place was fairly large, a big blockhouse with benches, plastic seats, and stained concrete walls. A flatscreen television that was far too small for the room played sitcoms in the corner.

She gestured toward the back, and he followed her into the locker area. It was free of other people, so she hurried to unlock two of the larger ones. Each held a duffel bag, green canvas army surplus, completely unidentifiable as ARES gear. Either Kayleigh or Deacon moved the bags to different bus stations monthly, again in an abundance of caution. *Or paranoia.*

They took the duffels to the house, dropped them off, and headed out again, this time by portal. An hour later, they were back at home with brand-new computers. He shook his head at the loss of his beloved computer setup and looked balefully at the off-the-shelf model in the box in front of him.

Then he shrugged it off. "We're alive, and we have gear and food. It's all good. Let's get this stuff organized. Hell, who knows, maybe we'll be locked down long enough to climb back onto the leaderboards in our game."

Kayleigh laughed. "Your skills have probably atrophied, what with all the work you've been doing."

He countered, "I haven't seen you put in much time, either. I'm still ten times as good as you are, even rusty."

She lifted an eyebrow. "Is that a challenge?"

He nodded. "Of course. Stakes?"

"Loser has to cook for a week."

"Deal. Let's get set up so I can kick your ass as soon as possible. I'm hungry."

CHAPTER SEVENTEEN

Cara's refuge, where she'd arrived after portaling out of the vimana, had turned out not to be much of one. She hadn't chosen a specific home like many of the others. Her life had mostly been rootless, a succession of bases and short-term rentals or long-term hotel stays as she moved around in the military. So it wasn't a total shock when she materialized in the forest behind a small motel in an equally small town to find that while the trees still stood, the building no longer did.

Instead, its former spot was now part of the parking lot for a retail store that had gone in on the main street, a few hundred feet away from the tree line. She'd been out of sorts about it for almost a full minute, not processing the sudden changes in her life effectively. Then she'd risen from her instinctive crouch and slapped her thighs., "All right, Cara. Get your shapely ass in gear."

She did have a storage garage in the small town, which was hopefully still standing. It was a walk of several miles to reach it, and she stayed in the forest where she could.

TR CAMERON

The trees and uneven terrain made it slow going, but time wasn't really a pressure at the moment. Her priorities were to get to a new safe spot and secure a burner phone before the scheduled check-in, and her destination would help with both of those.

She climbed over the fence and dropped into the rear of the self-storage facility, laughing inwardly at how similar it was to the location of her team's last mission. She slid up the door to the half-size garage and walked inside, pulling the barrier back down behind her. The push light was still where she'd left it, and its long-term batteries still functioned.

The dim illumination revealed a motorcycle with a dark helmet hanging from the handlebar. The space also held an air pump, oil, and gasoline to feed the machine. An old army friend of hers swapped out the fluids every three months to ensure they were fresh-ish. The other woman owed her from their time together in the field, and Cara trusted her with her life. *Literally, I guess, since if she gave up this location, I could wind up dead.*

She grabbed the pair of phones that lay on one of the shelves and cut them out of their packaging with a knife from the small toolkit inside the bike's pannier. It wasn't her favorite motorcycle ever, a used Kawasaki Vulcan touring model. It was the right choice for distance travel. One of her oldest leather jackets, frayed at the elbows and weather-beaten from its dark brown to more of a mottled tan, hung on a hook in the back, and she shoved the phones into its pockets.

Cara checked the pannier on the opposite side of the toolkit. It still contained her essential gear: a money belt

136

filled with bills of all denominations and an unregistered pistol with no identifying marks. Her chosen weapon was a revolver because it had fewer points of failure than an automatic. She loaded it from the string of bullets inside its case and stuck it back in the compartment, reluctantly adding her daggers and weapons belt since they were too obvious to wear. She locked up the pannier with the key to the bike.

She checked the tire pressure, topped off the fluids, and hit the starter. It took a couple of tries, but the engine eventually caught, filling the room with its throaty rumble. She pulled on her helmet, then exited the garage, locked it, and rolled out onto the nearest road, headed for another town she knew well.

It took three hours to reach her destination, but when she rode into the small town of Cusseta, Georgia, it felt like she'd never left. She was taking a risk, going back to a place that figured so prominently in her history, but she hoped that it would seem too obvious, and no one would believe she'd go to ground there.

Her first stop was at the strip mall at the edge of town, which held a Goodwill thrift store. She wandered through, searching the racks until she found stuff that she could live with, then headed to the restroom in the back.

She pulled the tags off the clothes as she changed into them, then put the clothes she'd worn into the store—tactical pants, black tank, and a heavy button-down shirt—onto the hangers. They went back on the racks, and she brushed past the cashier without stopping. She dropped the tags and a couple of twenties, more than enough to cover it, on the counter as she breezed by.

The woman who'd entered had looked vaguely military. The one who exited was in tight acid-washed jeans, a bright crop top that showed off her muscled stomach, oversized sunglasses, and a baseball hat embroidered with the word *Pink*. It was nothing like what she would've worn normally, and she spent a moment thinking that it was good Hank wasn't around to see it, or the jokes would never end.

She put a little extra bounce into her step. *If I get some gum and chew it aggressively, I might be able to pass for one of the women in Grease.* She laughed to herself. *I bet Anik would appreciate this look, though.*

Cara attached the helmet to the back of her bike, her current persona not likely to wear one despite the state's rule to the contrary. The girl in the hat probably wouldn't ride this particular motorcycle either, so she'd have to get it under cover before too long. That didn't pose a serious problem. This town, like the other she'd chosen, had most of what she'd need within walking distance of the hotel, including another self-storage space where she could rent a spot for her ride.

A couple of hours later, she closed the door to her hotel room. She'd paid for it in advance with cash—not an uncommon occurrence in this part of this particular town, which had military families coming in and out on a very regular basis—and walked toward another store she knew. She'd ridden by earlier in the day to make sure it was still there, taking a lesson from the disappearance of her first-choice motel, but it persevered.

She removed the hat and glasses as she entered Ray's Discount Army-Navy Surplus and nodded at the owner.

The man behind the counter was in his sixties but trim, muscular, and with the unique bearing of a drill sergeant. In fact, he'd been one. More specifically, he'd been hers.

Recognition blossomed in his eyes, but taking a cue from her outfit, he said, "Welcome to the shop, stranger. Anything I can do for you?"

She nodded. "Looking to pick up the essentials."

He gestured toward the shop, which had a handful of other customers inside, some probably ex-military and others looking like teenagers shopping for ways to annoy their parents. "Whatever you need, I'm sure we have it. Anything you don't find, ask."

She nodded and moved through the store casually, not going directly to the items she sought but acutely aware of the passage of time and how long the diminishing interval between the current moment and their assigned check-in time was. Having only the clothes on her back and not planning to need the disguise she was in for much longer, she picked out classic stuff that wouldn't attract attention in the military town.

When she finished, she had an armful. It included several pairs of khaki tactical pants and t-shirts with Army, Navy, and Marines emblazoned on them, enough for a week plus a day between washing. She also had several dress uniform tops in different colors, sufficiently heavy to keep her warm if that became an issue. She grabbed a web belt as she passed it, along with some pouches and a canteen to attach to it.

Cara stopped at an unmarked door near the back and stood on her tiptoes to look over the racks at the owner. He nodded, and the lock gave a soft *click*. She moved through it quickly, closing it behind her. This was the part of the store you only got access to if you already knew it was there. Bayonets and machetes rested on shelves climbing one wall, but she wouldn't need those as long as she had her daggers.

I do need something other than the revolver, though. Bull—once she mustered out, she was given the honor of using his name rather than his rank—wasn't willing to break the law in a big way, so he didn't carry guns. Instead, the room held heavy-duty Tasers, along with canisters of mace and pepper spray. She took a couple of each, then grabbed a police nightstick, technically a tonfa, wadding them all up inside the clothes filling her arms.

She used the eyehole in the door to time her exit, slipping out when the coast was clear. The walk to the counter resulted in a handful of protein bars added to the load. He rang up each item separately, moving the secret ones under the cover of the t-shirts. He named a number, and she handed over the requisite amount of bills. Quietly, he asked, "You okay?"

She nodded. "You know it. But if anyone asks, I wasn't here."

He packed her belongings in a duffel bag he'd thrown in for free, military surplus, of course, and set it on the counter. "Nope. You weren't. Haven't seen you in years, whoever the hell you are." He smiled. "If you need to 'not be here' again, come by anytime."

"Hooah, Sarge. Until then."

CHAPTER EIGHTEEN

Kevin Serrano strode into his team's shiny new offices for only the second time, and his sense of satisfaction was as keen as it had been on the first. His direct subordinate, Tash, was waiting inside the door, doubtless having watched his progress through the tracker in his car and the exterior cameras mounted surreptitiously on the facade of the office park building.

Their facility was small, more or less a cube that was three floors high. Two of them merged in the back to create a garage with a training area for his team. The space above it housed their main meeting area. The front of the building contained individual offices, smaller conference rooms, a kitchen, and the usual business stuff. After exchanging greetings with the witch, they walked to his office, where he held his palm against a sensor outside to unlock the door.

His desk was corporate casual, as was all the furniture in their space. No one, least of all him, had cared about any of those details. He only needed a functional place. Form didn't enter into it.

Tash, officially Natasha Kline, plopped down in the chair across from him and put her feet up on the desk. "So, what's the deal, Bossman?"

Kevin chuckled. During their first few months together, he'd tried reining in her attitude, which he'd initially judged unprofessional. It hadn't taken him much time to conclude that as long as her actions were professional and effective, which they were, he didn't care about her manners. "The senators were impressed with the vimana. They said so after you left. Not real thrilled we failed to capture any of the agents, though."

She shrugged. "Stuff happens. They had a good plan and executed it well. We're lucky to have gotten what we did."

"Agreed. I told the senators as much. They're politicians, though, so they probably only understood every third word and spent the whole conversation thinking about how to get a donation out of me."

Her laughter showed that her opinion of politicians matched his. "Well, at least the glad-handing is over for a while, right? They don't need you there to wipe their noses for them until something else major develops?"

He nodded. "If there's any mercy in heaven, that'll be awhile. Now, what's your take on our initial op?"

Tash straightened in her chair, dropping her boots to the floor. "The team worked well as a unit. Everyone did what they were supposed to. The anti-magic backpacks held Makka and me back, but that's fine. We knew we wouldn't have our normal abilities going in. That's what target practice is for."

He nodded. Making the magicals cross-train had been his idea, although he hadn't had a specific purpose for it when he'd told them to do it.

She continued, "I don't think we could've done anything better. The assault seemed to achieve total surprise, given how much stuff they left behind, especially the artifacts. They did some good contingency planning, executed the plan efficiently, and it worked out well for them. Not a damn thing anyone can do against that."

"Too true. How did the team take it?"

The witch laughed. "They went out for drinks that night and celebrated their total success, Makka tells me."

The unit hierarchy was pretty simple. He was in charge, Tash second in command. Together, they constituted the officer corps. The rest were under them, including the wizard who'd worked with Tash on countless other occasions. They could count on Makka to report truthfully on the actions of the others. It wasn't that Kevin didn't trust his people. He just believed in verification whenever possible.

He stifled a yawn and made a mental note to install a coffeemaker in his office. "And the rest of our base here?"

"Offices are assigned. We have a few rooms devoted to bunks in case we need to sleep over. Kitchen is fully stocked. Armory is in good shape, next to the garage, so we'll have no delays rolling out. Gun ranges are great for pistols but only okay for rifles. Too short. But you can't have everything."

"Outstanding. I'll be sure to kick that problem up the

ladder to our oversight committee, who will doubtless take it up as their primary concern."

He managed to put the perfect amount of sarcasm into the sentence to inspire a laugh from his subordinate. "How *is* that committee?"

He sighed. "A bunch of chuckleheads. Still, since the two senators from Nevada who are very clearly on our side lead it, I don't see too much trouble coming from the group. We might occasionally have to give one of them the dollar tour, let them wear a uniform, shoot a gun, that sort of thing. As long as our reports look right, I don't think they'll hassle us."

She lifted an eyebrow. "I noticed you specifically said, 'look right.' That's rather different from 'are right.'"

"It is. We'll take an 'honesty optional' approach with those folks. We tell them what we want them to know and keep back the things they might not be comfortable with. I'll be sure to feed the two at the top some extra information, but they still probably won't have the whole picture."

"Is that wise?"

Now it was his turn to laugh. "Honestly, I don't know if it is, but it's the only way we'll manage to get anything done. Far too many cooks trying to crowd into the kitchen for an op like this. Looks good on the resume to say you hunted down some traitors."

Tash nodded with a completely serious expression. "That's exactly why I'm here. Figured it would open up the job opportunities later."

He laughed at her dry delivery. "Sure, sure. My earlier warning still stands. Leave me, and I'll have you killed."

She returned the laugh. "Yeah, whatever boss. I'd fry you to a cinder before you had the chance."

"So I'll use a sniper rifle." He stood. "On that comradely note, get everyone together in the conference room. Time to switch from looking backward to looking forward."

It took about a half-hour to get the whole team in place because a couple of members were out to lunch. For the moment, they were operating as normally as possible, treating the job as a regular nine to five with some added moments of excitement here and there. That would have to change in short order, though, since their quarry had escaped and gone to ground.

Kevin paced in what he called the green room. The small office next to the conference room provided a nice view of the wooded area in the rear of the office park. *It would've been so much better if we'd been able to catch them all, or, hell, at least one of them. Would've looked better, would've provided a source of intel. Especially if it was the computer bastard.*

He shook his head. That person had done their job exceedingly well, leaving no useful shreds of data behind.

They'd only been aware of a couple of potential locations the unit's members might run to. Local FBI had been watching them from before the attack at his request, but they'd reported no activity. So, for the moment, those folks were still keeping an eye on them. The files on most of the agents hadn't provided any particularly likely destinations for them to run to, so they were more or less at ground zero, aside from continuing surveillance on obvious contacts.

That's fine. Sheen and her team are in a worse position than we are. He laughed inwardly. *It must've come as one hell of a shock to have their precious hidden base in freaking* Antarctica *invaded.*

He'd read through Sheen's file so many times he felt like he'd lived with her. Same with her boss, Bryant Bates, who had also evaded the government's efforts to snag him. That operation had been against his better judgment. He'd told the people above him to wait and keep quiet surveillance on the ARES boss, but they'd decided differently.

Well, maybe next time they'll listen to me, with the wisdom of experience. His focus now was finding the agents in the wind and bringing them in, if possible. If not, putting them down was a less desirable but entirely valid option.

He got a text message from Tash stating that the others were ready. He squared his shoulders, opened the door, and strode through. "Let me say it again. Well done, people. I mean that. We took their base with no losses, which is a total win.

"The fact that they had an excellent contingency plan in place for dealing with an invasion isn't a mark against us. If anything, it underscores how skilled our team was to overcome it without taking major injuries." A couple of the faces seated around the long conference table had looked nervous as he entered, but they slid into relaxed confidence at his words.

He sat at the head of the table and leaned his elbows on its surface. "So, now it's time to talk about how we move forward from here. We have surveillance on potential hideouts where we know about them. Either these people didn't have complete files to begin with, or they've been well-scrubbed. I think the latter, given how good their computer person is."

The tech expert on his team, Cassandra, interrupted. "We're pretty sure he's an infomancer. His file didn't say so, but some of the data had magic about it." She was only human but was nonetheless fantastic at what she did. *Her long red hair and pale skin are easy on the eyes, too.*

Kevin nodded. "That explains a lot. Marry great tech with magic, and it can be a bitch to overcome. That illustrates how unreliable our records on Sheen's team are. Clearly, from the start, either Sheen, Bates, or both have been holding back information. The discovery of more artifacts in their vault than they'd reported confirms that, and we know they got away with even more because of the empty boxes."

He shook his head, letting his frustration with how much latitude their foes had enjoyed fade. It didn't escape his attention that he was taking every bit as much leeway, but obviously, those two had deserved less, given how they'd behaved. "Okay, final thoughts or debriefs on the mission?"

Tash said, "In future missions, where possible, we should probably keep the anti-magic backpacks away from Makka and me."

"Definitely. We'll adapt our plans to that. This first one happened too quickly." His group had been together for less than a week before circumstances threw them into action. They'd received an indication that someone had breached their project's security, and they didn't want to give Sheen's team enough time to react if that was true.

Kevin rose and placed his palms on the table, leaning forward to meet each person's eyes in turn. "Here's what we're going to do. One, we're going to research the hell out of these people yet again. See if we can figure out where they might've gone.

"Tash and Makka will help with transport, and you'll put boots on the ground in any place that looks like it has possibilities. We're now pretty much operating a manhunt. And womanhunt. Think *The Fugitive* or *U.S. Marshals*."

Nods came from around the table as he continued, "Since we need to run these bastards down as quickly as possible before they can find their footing, item two is to distribute their pictures to the media and set up a tip line. Run that through the FBI. If we're lucky, the public will handle flushing them out for us. Any questions?"

None came, and he dispatched them to their tasks. He headed back to his office to dig into the history of the organization Sheen had been a part of. *Maybe I can figure out when and why she decided to turn traitor. That'll help me know what she's going to do next.*

CHAPTER NINETEEN

Kayleigh said, "I'm ready over here. How about you?" Deacon was sitting across from her at the dining room table, which they'd piled with computer gear they'd been wiring up for the past hour. "I think I'm ready, too. Okay, let me juice this thing."

She laughed inwardly. She loved how he described using his magical link with computers. Right now, he would use it to mask their hack into a local Internet Service Provider's line, wirelessly of course, and to activate a voice chat room he'd created on a Russian server long before. He'd said it was one located in a nuclear missile silo, but she never knew whether to believe him or not when he made claims like that.

Hell, I don't accept half the things I can verify because I figure he's probably faked verification information, too. His hands moved, but his eyes were closed, his magic somehow providing an interface with the system. She didn't understand, and she didn't need to. Finally, he said, "All right, we're good."

She logged onto the server and launched the chat room. For almost thirty nervous seconds, it was only her and her boyfriend in there. Deacon wouldn't interact much. His role was to monitor everything, ensuring no one was trying to trace them through their communication. It was exceedingly unlikely anyone could unless they were doing so from the user's end. No reason existed for anybody to be looking at the Russian server at all, at least not outside of Russia.

Then her heart leapt a little as others popped on. Protocol was not to speak until two minutes after the room had opened, so she waited, despite desperately wanting to know who users two, three, and so on were. Finally, the time came. She said, "Glam. Alice."

"Deke, Mad Hatter."

The next user announced, "Boss, Gandalf. Rambo, Frodo. Bark, Samwise."

She sighed in relief as Diana, Rath, and Max checked in. The book and movie references were a conditional code. Certain characters meant things were fine. Others signaled the user was under duress. They'd never written down the information, only discussed it verbally in secure spaces.

The rest checked in, one by one. "Face, Frankenstein." "Croft, Adler." "Khan, Scotty." "Hercules, Paul Atreides." "Class, Bond. James Bond." "Stark, I'll be your huckleberry."

Everyone laughed as Tony finished the cycle with the quote from *Tombstone*. Kayleigh breathed, "Thank heaven." She looked up, and Deacon nodded. "Deke says the room is secure."

Diana said, "We're fine, primary location. Status?"

Khan replied, "I'm pretty sure someone's watching me. I

haven't been outside or anything, but there are some government-looking sedans parked nearby. Maybe FBI. I could simply be paranoid. I've put out a bunch of surprises for anyone who tries to break in here."

"Need one of us to come get you?"

"No. Not yet. If I do, I'll send the signal."

Hank said, "I'm safe. Primary location. I'd like to go get the truck, though."

Everyone laughed, and Kayleigh replied, "Well, of course, you would." The rolling battleship of an eighteen-wheeler was his pride and joy, and he hadn't gotten the chance to use it very often since their last night in Pittsburgh.

Diana crushed his hopes, as Kayleigh had known she would. "Sorry, Hercules, but our enemies will *definitely* be watching that. It's on the record. My guess is they'll keep it safe and sound for us, hoping we'll drop by to pick it up. So, until we really need it, not an option."

Cara asked, "Will it be safe from them?"

He laughed. "It's keyed only to open for one of us. Sure, they could cut their way inside, but I also set it for self-defense. The AIs would stop that attempt in its tracks. I don't think anyone's getting in there, not without disassembling it from the ground up with robots they're willing to replace."

Tony drawled, "Primary location. All good. Sunshine is a nice change."

Sloan said, "Stepped into some old shoes. Reactivating some past contacts. Hoping I can figure out what's going on here."

Bryant replied, "Let's coordinate on that before we

leave here. I have some people you should reach out to and a list of those to avoid. Also, safe at primary."

"Sounds good."

Cara said, "I had to go to my secondary. Primary wasn't there anymore, which was a bit of a surprise. I'm good for the moment, but I should probably stay on the move."

Kayleigh asked, "Need assistance?"

"Nah, I'm good. If I need help, though, I'll call for it, believe me."

She said, "You better. Deke had to abandon his primary, too. He's with me. We had a couple of setbacks, but nothing we couldn't cope with. Everything's fine now."

Diana asked, "You're sure?"

Kayleigh appreciated the extra note of worry in her voice. They shared a lot of history, and those moments where Diana unconsciously reaffirmed their connection mattered to her. She wasn't willing to do the work to psychoanalyze *why* they mattered. It was enough to know her boss cared about her as more than an everyday employee. *Of course, I'm sure she feels that way about everyone on the team.* "No. We're good."

Diana said, "Okay, then. I presume y'all have seen that we're TV stars now, right?"

Both affirmatives and negatives sounded in response. Kayleigh sighed. "Not only TV. Radio, Internet, probably tomorrow's newspapers. Pictures, descriptions. A great big 'be on the lookout.' They specifically used the T-word for you, boss."

Sloan asked, "T-word?"

Diana replied, "Terrorist. Apparently, the fact that we

didn't turn over as many artifacts as we should've has pissed somebody off, big time."

Tony said, "That's what this is all about? Damn, government agencies lie a hundred times a day. Why should we be held to a different standard?"

Bryant answered, "Theoretically, we shouldn't. Practically, lots of reasons. Our mandate is to deal with magicals, which still scares the hell out of most government people. Plus, they think Diana's betrayed their trust. Of course, given the surveillance that must've been going on for quite a while to figure that out, there wasn't all that much trust in the first place."

Diana asked, "Can we go to Johnston? Is he still in our corner?"

Kayleigh had never met the senator but knew he was the one who'd hooked them up with the base in Antarctica, a mysterious figure at the center of a lot of stuff where magic met politics. Bryant replied, "In the wind, near as I can tell. At the very least, he hasn't stuck his head up since this happened. We should count ourselves lucky to have anyone in the government on our side, I suppose."

Diana said, "We should assume we can't fully trust anyone other than the people in this room. Server. Thing. Whatever." Kayleigh stifled a laugh as the other woman continued speaking. "We continue to follow the Zulu scenario by the numbers until I say different. That way, we know what everyone is up to.

"If you have to deviate for the sake of safety, do it, and let me know. The worst thing for the whole team right now is if one of us gets caught. That gives them leverage, even though we'd like to think we'd all be strong enough not to give in if they captured a colleague. Plus, there's no telling what magic or drugs they can use to get secrets out of people nowadays. So, staying out of their hands is key."

Hercules asked, casually, "How serious about that do you want us to be, Boss?"

Even Kayleigh, who spent very little time in the field, understood the subtext of his question. Diana replied, "We stay nonlethal in all circumstances, right up until the moment where it's kill or be killed. I suppose it would be better to be captured than for any of us to wind up with a murder rap." Silence filled the channel for a moment as everyone considered the weight of what she'd said.

Tony remarked, "Well, then, I'll have to pick up something less lethal than my pistol." The others made similar comments, and a few laughs and jokes were traded, especially toward Tony. They suggested he buy a Nerf gun since he was a good enough shot that he could still probably render someone unconscious with it.

As the conversation wrapped up, Diana said, "We'll come through this, and we'll be together again. Then we'll figure out what's going on and set things right. Count on it. Until then, people, stay safe."

Everyone gave those two words as their farewells as they left the room until it was only Kayleigh and Deacon remaining. She whispered, "Stay safe, all of you," then shut down the virtual space. Looking over at her boyfriend, she said, "Time for us to do some digging."

CHAPTER TWENTY

For Cara, running scenario Zulu by the books held an additional obligation not shared by most of the team. Only one other, in fact, Hank, who would doubtless be on the move already. Her destination was a four-hour drive from her location and longer for him, so she had time to visit the surplus store again and gather some outdoor clothes, a camouflage jacket, a sleeping bag, and a tent.

The drill sergeant behind the counter asked, "Hunting?"

Cara smiled. "Of a sort."

"You keep yourself safe."

"Will do, Bull."

She carried the bundle to the self-storage place, then pulled out her bike and arranged the new purchases on it. She didn't anticipate needing to use the stuff, but if something delayed Hank, it might be better to stay completely off the radar by camping rather than booking a hotel room. Kicking the motorcycle into gear, she rolled out.

As she rode, her mind was in two places at once. One part of it was able to enjoy the moment, the feel of the wind pressing against her, the sight of the scenery going by, even the scents from the occasional vehicle she passed on the back roads. None of that had been part of her life at the vimana, and it was a pleasant change. The rest of her brain tumbled through potential plans and outcomes for the op ahead and didn't like much of what occurred to her.

Her task was to visit their backup base and ensure it was still operational. The fundamental assumption of scenario Zulu was that someone had deeply compromised them. Diana had made the split-second decision to choose the most distrusting of the defense options, and Cara had learned not to doubt her boss's instincts on such matters. The alternate home for the team was a bunker in an abandoned army facility, long since closed, which was fine in itself.

The problem lay in that they hadn't done the retrofit to turn it into an alternate base themselves. Various military engineering groups had outfitted it under the guise of training, sensibly calling it an emergency fallback location for military command in case of an invasion.

She'd thought the rationale was thin, but Bryant's contacts had assured him they commonly used such stories to keep the people performing the engineering projects focused. Sure, the trainees suspected it was nonsense, but they also had a concrete goal to concentrate on.

Of course, the build had been thoroughly checked out by engineers *not* in training when the construction was complete and was deemed viable. Over time, they portaled in equipment, turning the bunker into a legit backup base for the team. The only thing it lacked was data. Deacon would bring that with him on hard drives containing their artificial intelligences and the records that were too sensitive to allow to exist anywhere except their very own computers.

An early suggestion had been to put the artifact vault there rather than the vimana, but Diana had refused. That had been the initial moment when Cara had realized the other woman was skirting the rules about the magical items. She still didn't fully understand why and would eventually have to broach the topic if the boss didn't do it first. *Second in command. Need the info*, she thought, channeling her inner Dr. Evil.

The problem was, all of that meant the base existed somewhere in the government's paperwork. From what they'd seen on the flash drive Bryant had given them, government records were far from secure when someone in that government was after them. *Kevin Serrano, whoever the hell that is. Jumped-up, suit-wearing bureaucrat, probably.*

She pulled over to refuel the bike and herself and put the SIM card into the prepaid cell phone, making it active. She found some music on the Internet and stuck a Bluetooth earbud in one ear, leaving the other free to hear traffic and other sounds. Then she climbed back on and headed for the rendezvous point.

When she arrived, she parked the bike in the corner of a grocery store parking lot and waited. She had no idea what Hank would be driving, but he would know she'd be on a motorcycle. That meant initiating contact was his responsibility.

After about ten minutes, the last two of which she spent debating whether to try to call him, a large van with tinted windows pulled up beside her. It was shiny black, except for a bright yellow trim that started as a double racing stripe on the hood, wrapped around the doors, the sides, and presumably the back, although she couldn't see that from her angle.

The window slid down to reveal Hank's smiling face. "Hey, gorgeous. Want to take a ride in my van?" He waggled his eyebrows, and Cara burst into genuine laughter. She and Hank had shared a great relationship from the moment they'd met, really like brother and sister, but with a frequent stream of innuendo and fake flirting.

Romance wasn't possible between them. They didn't like each other that way. Goofing around while they sparred or were on a mission was totally legit. Anik had asked her about their wordplay once, and she'd explained there wasn't a spark, ever. Only deep trust and platonic affection. She didn't know if he'd believed it, but that was his problem to deal with, not hers.

She locked down her bike and grabbed the important stuff from her panniers, plus the camping gear, and moved around to the back of the van. He opened the rear doors from inside, and she saw that the vehicle had six bucket seats and enough room behind them for several people to sit on the floor. Right now, the storage area held a couple of duffels and a pile of camping equipment. She shook her head. "Great minds think alike."

He held out a hand and pulled her up into the van after she grabbed it. "Wasn't sure what we'd find. Figured having as many options as possible was the best policy."

"Agreed." She settled into the passenger seat and buckled her seatbelt. "Wait for dark?"

He nodded. "Smartest move."

"Okay, drop me off at the front door. I'll get us snacks." Hank grinned. "Now that's what I call a good plan."

When full darkness fell, the van was parked a mile away from the bunker, on the far side of a large swath of woodland from the base. Hank had brought along commercial grade night vision goggles used by hunters, and they made good time through the forest. When they stopped at the edge of the tree line, their destination was about two hundred feet away, guarded by a barbed wire, chain-link fence. Signs warned of electrical shock, but those were lies. *At least they were the last time we were here.*

They stayed low, crouching as they moved through the tall grass to the fence. It held no telltale buzz of electricity, and Hank snapped the links with a small, motorized bolt cutter. She whispered, "You have the right tool for every job, don't you?"

He laughed. "All the ladies say so."

Cara sighed. "Walked straight into that one, didn't I?"

Hank laughed again. "That's another perfect setup, but I'm gonna let it go. We need to be mission-focused, right?"

"Right."

They reached the front door, which was locked, naturally. Lifting a disguised panel revealed eight buttons they needed to push in a certain sequence. They'd all memorized the code, as well as the one that would lock it from all outside access. When she entered the correct numbers, the door unlatched. "So far, so good."

He nodded and pulled it open enough that they could

get through. She went in first, and he closed it behind them. Motion sensors detected their presence and emergency lights around them illuminated to show the entry room. A desk sat in the front, where a receptionist would sit. As if they would need that in their base. *I guess it's a useful part of the cover story. Generals wouldn't want to be bothered.*

She rolled her eyes and headed for the single door that left the space. She looked up at the globes mounted on the ceiling at the back corners of the room. Inside each was a turret that, if the facility were in defensive mode, would deploy and hose down any hostile attempting to enter with a liberal stream of bullets.

Those systems were down at the moment, thankfully. It would take time and effort to bring the bunker's systems online, and the fact that they were down reassured her that *maybe* their enemies hadn't yet discovered this particular piece of information about the team. *Once we establish ourselves in here, any enemy will have a hell of a job ahead of them trying to root us out.*

They made their way through the facility, heading for the control center and the armory behind it. Cara's hands were itching to get some better weapons than the ones she carried, other than Angel and Demon, which were currently in modified shoulder holsters under her jacket. They'd wanted to have at least the appearance of being civilians if the police or another authority had stopped them, so they'd come in wearing camouflage and carrying typical hunting rifles. She was sure Hank had a pistol on him somewhere, though, as she did.

When they reached the control center, she breathed a

sigh of relief. "I expected to find a whole battalion in here waiting for us."

He nodded. "Me too. Guess we lucked out."

She grinned. "Guess so."

With a buzzing flicker, the lights in the room came fully to life, and the various control panels started to glow. She snapped, "Hey, premature illumination there, buddy."

His voice held only concern as he ignored her innuendo. "Wasn't me."

"Shit. Grab some weapons and let's get the hell out of here. Clever bastards. Let us make it all the way in before springing their trap."

CHAPTER TWENTY-ONE

C ara bolted into the armory a step ahead of Hank. She reached out with her telekinesis to pull a rifle off the wall, and her power failed to come. "Damn and double damn them. Anti-magic emitters."

Her partner growled, "Well, of course. Didn't want us simply portaling out of here."

She took the steps over to the weapons rack, grabbed the carbine, and yanked it down. "I swear by all things holy, when I find out who's behind all this, I'll kick him so hard his family jewels will fly out of his mouth."

Hank laughed. "There's the Cara I know and love."

"Lock down the hormones there, buddy."

He offered a grin that completely ignored the situation they were in. "You know what they say. Danger amps up your senses. Could be hot."

She grabbed a combat shotgun from the rack, turned, and threw it at him. He effortlessly snatched it out of the air with another laugh. She popped the magazines from two other rifles, shoving them in her jacket pockets. Then she turned, pulled the coat off, and snagged one of their custom bulletproof vests from the shelf.

Hank was next to her in a moment, doing the same after setting a Glock 17 pistol and extra magazine beside her. "Upgrade."

She managed a smile through her anger. "Thanks, man." She finished putting on her vest, pulled on shock gloves, and joined the lines that connected the two. If anyone blasted her with lightning, the gloves would instantly charge. Unfortunately, the batteries were all reading dead since the power hadn't been on in the room. She looked forlornly at the open spot on the vest where an anti-magic deflector would normally be, then grabbed her jacket and zipped it up.

An equipment belt was next. She strapped the holster to her thigh and shoved the pistol into it. *Who needs batteries? I have a pistol, rifle, extra mags, and Angel and Demon. Time to kick some tail.*

Hank finished clicking shells into the holders attached to the shotgun. It held eight in the drum, but he had to reload it by hand. The tradeoff was that the ammunition was far more powerful than off-the-shelf models. Cara noted he'd selected the blue ones. "Remaining nonlethal in the situation is gonna suck."

"Agreed. I'll take out whoever I can with these stun rounds. Which I guess means I'm on point."

"Yeah. I knew getting into the armory was too good to be true."

He laughed. "Always the case. Never trust a gift. You ready?"

Cara ordered, "Move." It took them five minutes of

careful creeping to reach the first floor of the bunker. The building's layout made infiltration as difficult as possible. That meant only one set of stairs connected the levels, positioned at maximum distances from other accesses.

The steps let them out at the rear of the facility, with several offices, storage areas, and open spaces between them and freedom. She tried to summon a small flame, found that her magic was still blocked, and complained, "These people suck."

Hank moved before her in a slow walk, the shotgun raised, his whole posture one of total attention to his surroundings. He didn't reply. *That's because he's in the zone, which is where you want to be. Get your shit together, Cara.*

She carried her rifle with the barrel toward the floor so if it went off unexpectedly, it wouldn't shoot her or her partner. She repeated in her mind the warning not to kill anyone. At this point, the accusations against her and Hank were false. Killing government or military agents would put them on the other side of a line they didn't want to cross.

The attack came as a surprise, which was impressive since they were waiting for it. As they crossed an intersection between closed office doors on either side, bullets pounded through the wooden barriers and into them. Hank dove forward with a shout, and Cara threw herself backward. Her arm and leg burned like she'd taken hits, but she had no time to worry about that.

The initial barrage more or less shredded the doors, and the turrets inside the offices were visible through what remained. She lifted the rifle and hosed down the one that was swiveling in her direction. She destroyed it an instant before she would have had to dive away from the stream of bullets it was bringing toward her. The blast of the shotgun, followed by the sizzle of the ammunition and a loud *bang* as the other turret detonated, indicated Hank was still in the fight. She muttered through gritted teeth, "I'm hit, but functional. You?"

His voice held more anger than pain, even though she thought he'd taken several rounds. "Same. Drink up."

She pulled the healing potion out of her jacket's interior pocket and drank it down, wincing as it pushed a bullet out of her leg. When the repair was complete, she said, "I have an extra if you need it.

He replied, "Might have to take you up on that. I took three rounds. Potion did most of the job, but not all of it. Hopefully, I can manage not to get hurt again."

"Guess we have to clear as we go." They'd hoped that speed would be their best defense, but that situation had changed.

"Affirmative."

She swapped magazines, and he reloaded, then they crept cautiously forward, opening each door they came to and engaging defenses where they were present.

The trap had been well-set. Some of the turrets were ground-level, others high up. A couple had launched grenades instead of bullets, gas-filled canisters that forced them to reroute, having neither gas masks nor the ability to use magic to contain the vapors. Cara asked, "Ever get the feeling you're a rat in a maze?"

"Totally. We can handle anything the mad scientists out there throw our way. Exit door is about thirty feet ahead if I remember right, one more turn between here and there."

He gestured at the corner in front of them. "Think we'll find a welcoming committee in the entry?"

"Could be. Got turrets in all four corners though, so maybe they're trusting the equipment to do the work."

He shook his head, and she heard the grin in his words. "You really shouldn't have activated the base. Everything was fine until then."

She scowled at him. "You're a moron."

Hank laughed as he reloaded the shotgun again. "You must be worried if that's the best you can come up with. Thoughts on how to defeat the turrets?"

"Take the far two from the hallway, then stick the guns around the sides and shoot at the nearer pair without exposing ourselves. I think it works most optimally if you stand right in front of me and I shoot around you."

"Not cool, Croft."

She laughed. "But you're so big."

He looked down at himself. "What do you know? Guess I am. That explains all the jealousy I get from y'all. I'll take left. You take right."

"Works for me." She swapped out her partially emptied magazine for a full one, then lifted the rifle to her shoulder. "Ready."

"Let's do it."

They rushed down the corridor, blowing by the turrets inside the offices they passed. Gas canisters landed in the hallway behind them. Cara held her breath in an abundance of caution as she stepped forward and fired at the turret in the far corner of the entry room, blasting it into pieces before it could adjust its angle enough to hit her. Hank did the same on the other side. Then they stuck their weapons around the edges, shooting blindly into the spots where the walls and ceiling met in the corners.

When the cacophony of the turrets' firing stopped, they crept carefully into the room. She tried again to access her magic and once more discovered that she couldn't. Hank shoved his last rounds into the shotgun. "Get outside, portal to the van?"

Cara shook her head. "They might have surveillance on it. Worse, they could be waiting for us there. We can't simply pop in without knowing if it's a trap. We should leave it."

Hank growled, "We are *not* leaving my van behind. Not an option."

"Seriously?"

"Some things are nonnegotiable. I'm not abandoning my van. If you can get away, you should."

A sigh escaped her as she made the only possible choice. "Hell no. We're partners. If you're going to be stupid, I guess we'll be stupid together."

He chuckled. "Won't be hard for you. You've had a lot of practice."

"You are, without a doubt, the most —

Hank interrupted, "Hold that thought. Let's go." He hit the button to open the front door and rushed outside.

CHAPTER TWENTY-TWO

When they'd entered the bunker, the large area in front had held nothing but overgrown grass. Now, two death machines stared at them from that expanse of green. The mechanical beasts had earned that name from the Army the first time the prototypes had deployed in the field. The units were intended for base defense and designed with two primary objectives: absorb incoming damage and wipe out scores of enemies at once with their offensive weapons.

She and Hank ran in opposite directions as the first rockets flew in, slamming into the bunker behind them and sending concrete shrapnel flying everywhere. She'd never trained against the things, had no knowledge of how to deal with them at all. *A grenade might work, although that heavy armor is a problem. It would have to detonate right on one of the weapons ports. Without my magic to guide it, I'm not that good. Plus, I don't have a grenade.*

The monoliths offered no visible vulnerabilities, only huge interlocking metal shields designed to absorb damage with occasional openings for offense. Behind the armor would be a big column filled with weapons, sensors, and other vital components. The death machines were incapable of relocating at any speed because of their tall cylindrical shape, by design, but were entirely lethal once in place.

Cara embraced her only reasonable option and ran like hell for the tree line. She tried calling up her magic as she pelted over the ground, but again, it wouldn't come. She growled under her breath, "Damn bastards and their bloody freaking anti-magic emitters. If there's one thing I detest, it's a level playing field, or worse, one tilted in the enemy's direction."

She angled through the hole Hank had made in the fence and went to ground in the woods, crouching against a tree and pulling a fallen branch across her body to break up her outline.

She waited, trying to calm her breathing, and devoutly wished they could risk using their comms. Even without the booster units they carried as part of their normal loadout, the small devices in their ears would've been enough to connect her and her partner. *The existence of the signals would probably give us away.*

A rustling came from behind her several minutes later, and she slowly shifted to aim her pistol at it. Then, at the edge of her hearing, the source of the noise said, "Okay, you were right. We should've portaled."

She softly laughed as Hank joined her. "We can't. Still have anti-magic going on."

"Must be backpacks, which means we have people nearby."

"Yeah. Those things in the front yard were a smart play. I'd guess they deliberately drove us to the forest. They probably could've gunned us down the moment we came through the door."

He muttered, "Hope my van's okay," and set the shotgun on the ground. "I'm empty."

"I'm embarrassed to say I lost count somewhere along the line. There are at least a few in each mag. Maybe keep yours as a club, though?"

He lifted his fists. "I have all the clubs I need right here, baby."

Cara shook her head, surprised to find herself smiling. "You know, you're certifiably insane."

The insult earned her a grin. "Yeah. I get that. Stay together or split up?"

"Together. You lead."

He moved out, and she followed carefully, putting her feet right where his went. They were both trained to notice traps, both experienced at being in the woods, and capable of handling anyone they might find in hand-to-hand combat. *As long as we don't get shot first.* He stopped suddenly, and she crept up close enough to whisper in his ear. "What you got?"

"Noise off to the left. Might've been deliberate. I'm guessing there's one up to the right, too."

"Okay. Sixty seconds."

"Good deal."

Hank moved stealthily through the forest, watching the ground before each step, then raising his gaze to check the area all around him. He was headed toward the noisemaker because they were sure that *something*, at least, was in this direction. In this particular situation, needing to remain nonlethal, he was more skilled than Cara, which didn't happen very often. *I guess all those nights at fight clubs paid off.*

He hadn't shared his hobby widely, but Cara knew. She'd needed to blow off steam at one point and wouldn't accept help from anyone, so he'd found her someone to fight. Things had gotten better after that, and whenever they flared up, another night out to blow off some steam solved the problem.

A whisper came from his left, and he altered his course. His target had apparently moved since making the first sound. *Makes sense. They're probably tightening the circle, creeping in toward the base. They'd best not be messing with my van.* He'd paid for the vehicle out of his pocket, and shortly after buying it was forced to abandon it when they relocated to the vimana. Now that they were reunited, he was eager to get going on the customization project he'd planned.

Hank was the type of person who couldn't relax unless he was building something, fixing something, or fighting something. He spotted the enemy, wearing camouflage with a helmet, a rifle, and one of the same backpacks seen on the base cameras during the invasion. The figure moved like it was comfortable in the woods, and Hank immediately assessed his target as a moderate threat, probably Special Forces.

In a standup conflict, he might've been more concerned, but he had no intention of giving the other person an opportunity to fight back. He slipped in beside him and wrapped an arm around his neck, gripping it tightly with his other hand and choking and squeezing. It would've been over in a second if he'd been able to kill the man, a crushed windpipe ending him, but instead, he had to wait while the lack of blood to the man's brain rendered him unconscious.

He quickly pulled the man's communication unit off and trussed him with his zip ties. Nothing presented itself as an easy solution to a gag, and Hank didn't want to risk punching him in the head. *Besides, if he does make noise, it might turn out to be a useful distraction.*

He rose and barely jerked back in time to avoid the rifle butt that whipped across in front of his face. The man's partner had apparently snuck up in complete silence while Hank was tying up his buddy. *Okay, some of these bastards are better than we thought.*

The newcomer shouted for help, and Hank popped him in the facemask to shut him up. The man took the blow and swiped the butt of his rifle back, reversing the path taken in the first attempt to bash his brains in. Hank got a hand up to block but still got knocked to the side as the rifle struck it.

He turned the stumble into a circle, darting in and kicking out at the other man's leg. His foe lifted his boot to block the kick, then launched a sidekick without setting the foot down.

Hank slapped it contemptuously aside, the blow not having enough power to make it worth the time it had cost.

He darted in and punched the man's ribs but encountered protective padding. He whipped an elbow at the side of the man's head, but his foe tilted his helmet down to take the shot. Hank's elbow ached from the impact, and he hoped the man's skull did as well.

Crashing sounds came from the left, signaling the potential for yet more enemies. He ran in the general direction of his van while muttering a steady stream of curses.

When her mental clock hit zero, Cara dashed forward at her opponent and swept his legs out from underneath him. He fell with a cry, and she punched him in the throat to shut him up, pulling the blow so it wouldn't do any real damage. She yanked off his helmet with a grab and a twist, then delivered a punch to his temple, again taking care to moderate the power of the strike.

A crashing to her right alerted her that another enemy was present, and she snarled in frustration. She ran toward it, hoping to get to whoever it was before they could put out an alarm.

Shouts came from the direction Hank had gone, and she mentally reviewed all the curses she knew. She reached her target as he yelled, in shock, alarm, or warning, she didn't know, and threw a punch at his face. He got his rifle in the way to knock her arm aside. She spun and delivered a back kick to his midsection that drove him a couple of steps backward, but he had armor, so that wouldn't be the end of the fight.

Cara reached under her coat and drew Angel and Demon, then reacquired her target. She threw Angel as he lifted the rifle, her right hand whipping forward and hurling the dagger blade-first into his near shoulder. His rifle chattered, but the shots went wide as he recoiled in pain. She raced at him and jumped into the air, kicking out at the damaged limb. He went down with a cry, clearly in agony from the wound, and she ripped the blade out, careful not to make the injury worse. She screamed, "Medic, medic over here, man down," then raced for where they'd left the van.

Bullets followed her as she smashed through branches and wove around trees. They'd set the trap *exceedingly* well, but their foes had overestimated the skills of the people in the forest or underestimated her and Hank. Either way, since the shots were coming primarily from behind, they'd made it to the outer cordon before engaging.

She burst from the trees and saw Hank already running to the driver's side of the van. She rushed to the passenger door, yanked it open, and jumped in. Without a word, he stomped on the accelerator and peeled out. She tried to make a flame again, and this time succeeded. He growled, "Back doors. Handholds on the roof."

She nodded and climbed down the space in the middle of the bucket seats, then threw the back door open while holding onto the grip he'd mentioned. When they reached the side road that connected the parking lot they'd been in to the main road, two vehicles sped up behind them. Cara grinned, remembering Rath's obsession with caltrops a month or so before. She summoned ice, formed it into spiky balls, and tossed them out onto the road.

When the trailing cars ran over them, the small objects shredded their tires, and they smashed into each other before stopping. She yanked the door closed and went back to the front of the van, settling in beside Hank with a laugh. "Well, that wasn't exactly fun."

He nodded. "I'll pull over as soon as we're a couple of miles away. They probably put a tracer on the van."

Cara shook her head. "You know, you should leave this thing behind."

"Never."

"It's only a car."

Hank stared at her, deliberately not looking at the road as he intoned, "If you keep talking, you'll force me to punch you."

She laughed and grinned widely. "Now *there's* the Hank I know and love."

CHAPTER TWENTY-THREE

B ryant was back in D.C. although people were looking for him, and if a single place existed where he was most likely to be recognized, Washington was it. *It's not like I'm going to sit here and do nothing while our enemies draw a cordon down around us.*

Frustratingly, Diana was following protocol, which meant she wasn't reaching out to him and thus he couldn't reach out to her, despite wanting more personal reassurance that she was okay. *If I'm able to find some useful information, it might get us to the point where we can be together faster.*

He'd always figured that if things went wrong, she'd be at his side, and vice versa. To have it fall out this way was downright irritating. *So, if I need another reason to be ticked off at whoever's behind this, I have one.*

All of that was why he was slowly walking down the street across from Aaron Finley's brownstone. As a matter of routine, he'd researched the man's regular schedule before all this happened so he could make contact anytime he wanted. He wore a suit, carried a briefcase, and looked nothing like himself. At the moment, he was using illusion to change his features.

The case held a few cosmetic disguise pieces in a hidden compartment he could employ if anti-magic emitters came into play. The coat over the suit was reversible, and while he wore a fashionable fedora, he had a knit cap in one pocket and a slouchy driver's hat in the other. It wasn't the best spy craft, but it would do. *Plus, it's all I have, so it will have to.*

Finley emerged within a minute of when he usually exited the house and got into the car waiting for him. Bryant kept walking, turned a corner, and summoned his ride. The driverless vehicle took him to the Senate building, and he got there in time to see Finley walk up the stairs toward the main entrance with a cup of coffee in each hand. He reliably, nine days out of ten, stopped to pick up a to-go cup from his favorite coffee shop for himself and his secretary.

Bryant sighed, wishing he'd had time to stop for coffee, then settled in for a long day of surveillance.

After a couple of hours, an app on his phone signaled for his attention. He hit the right buttons and popped one of the phone's earbuds into his left ear. Sloan's voice came to him. "Heading inside now. Anything you need me to check?"

Bryant chuckled. "Who are you today?"

"Kyle Strang, lobbyist for a group of small biotech firms. Not surprisingly, I was able to put together a bunch of meetings real fast. I managed to get some from both sides of the aisle, which is a notable change. The last time I did this, the Democrats weren't interested."

"Everybody wants money, especially these days."

"Too true. The kicker is, I think I might manage to do some deals. That's going to come as a major surprise to the biotech firms involved, but I imagine they'll be grateful."

Bryant shook his head in moderate disbelief. Their unit's best spy, Sloan, was equal parts con man and intelligence agent. He could be anyone at the drop of a hat. They'd had evenings out where he'd blended seamlessly from personality to personality, chosen more or less at random by using the people in the bar or restaurant as inspiration. He always had the table crying with laughter by the time he finished.

"Stop in unannounced on Senator Finley, if you'd be so kind, and let me know if he's in his office. Other than that, maybe see if you can get an appointment with either of the senators from Nevada."

"Right into the lion's den, eh? Sure, will do. Gotta go for a bit." The connection closed, and Bryant switched over to an audiobook and hit play. *There are worse ways to spend a day than relaxing amid the hustle and bustle of government and listening to* The Martian.

About half the time, Finley left his office and went directly to a restaurant in the blocks surrounding the capital buildings for dinner. Tonight was one of those occasions, and Bryant followed as the senator and an unknown man walked to their destination. Finley had often complained to him about the difficulty of finding time to exercise, so he tended to walk whenever possible. *Which isn't the best thing for him, safety-wise, but works in my favor at the moment.*

He morphed his features along the way and turned his jacket inside out in case either of the men might have sensed a presence trailing them. They went into a restaurant, and he entered another whose windows looked out onto the street so he could keep an eye on the door that had swallowed up his quarry. He ate quickly and was outside before Finley emerged.

Bryant watched as the senator's car pulled up, then hailed one to follow. Forty minutes later, they were both back where they'd started, him outside the brownstone and Finley inside. Bryant changed hats, flipped his coat again, and headed down the street.

His initial idea had been to march up and knock on the door, but if Finley were under surveillance, that would be too dangerous. Instead, he walked around the block and came in from the back of Finley's house.

The windows on the first two stories had bars over them, ornate and attractive, but still an effective defense. He summoned his telekinesis to unlatch an upper window and slide it open, then used force magic to launch himself up to the ledge. He crawled inside, climbing quietly to the floor, and closed the window behind him.

Finley's voice came as a surprise. "Turn around real slow. Any sudden movements and you're going to find yourself bleeding from way more holes than you want to have in your body."

He froze, then laughed. "Is that any way to treat an old friend, Aaron?"

A few minutes later, they were seated at the senator's kitchen table, and Finley was shaking his head. "You're an idiot; you know that? I could've shot you."

Bryant nodded. "I will admit, I didn't expect you to have a shotgun. Figured you more as a Taser kind of guy."

His host replied, "Tasers can't do much against a Kilomea or giant troll if they decided to come inside. The world is strange."

"It is indeed. I hate to break it to you, but that shotgun wouldn't do more than irritate a Kilomea or troll."

Finley sighed. "I know. I just like the shotgun, okay?"

Bryant lifted a hand. "Not here to judge."

"Why *are* you here?" The other man tipped another measure of bourbon into both of their glasses. "Probably easier and safer ways for you to arrange a meet."

"What do you know about Kevin Serrano?"

The other man swirled his bourbon, looking down into it as if the answer was inside. "I figured that's what this was about. Not much, I'm afraid. He's a rising star, though it's unclear exactly where he rests in the government organizational chart."

Bryant frowned and sipped his drink. "Which is weird, right?"

"Totally weird. Usually, he gives off the impression he's with the FBI. Maybe that's true, but I don't think so. I think his outfit is truly independent, even more so than yours. Probably empowered by some secret document that'll never see the light of day with a specific purpose."

He scowled. "Hunting down my team."

Finley nodded once. "And you. Don't leave yourself out. You're an important part of the picture, too."

"This is a damn convoluted way to address what they saw as a problem. I would've been willing to talk to Diana, maybe."

The other man tapped the table with a finger. "Not from what I hear."

He frowned and met his host's eyes. "Which is?"

"That Sheen's a wildcard, and you were too busy sleeping with her to keep her in check."

He wasn't quite kidding when he replied, "Say something like that to me again, and you're gonna need that shotgun, Aaron."

The senator leaned back and held up both hands. "I surrender. Mea culpa. I'm telling you what I heard, that's all."

"Any idea where I find the chuckleheads in charge?"

"No doubt you know where the Nevada senators are. You're not going to accomplish anything with them. Serrano and his team are like ghosts, as near as I can tell. Not that I've tried to delve too deep since I don't want to wind up on the target list with you. I wouldn't be able to help you, then," he finished with a small smile.

He laughed. "Sure, that's the reason."

Finley nodded. "I'm not secret agent material. We already knew that."

"We did. However, you're excellent at what you do. Can you find me a place to start looking?"

"I think so. Give me a day."

"Good deal."

Finley met his eyes. "Bryant?"

"Yes?"

The other man grinned. "Pick up the phone next time. I'd hate to shoot you by accident."

CHAPTER TWENTY-FOUR

Kevin Serrano emptied his magazine into the target, then released it, letting it fall past his other hand as it pushed in another mag. He emptied that one into the target as well, scowling at the unusually wide spread of his shots.

He took off the ear protectors with a snarl. From behind him, Tash observed, "Not your best work, boss. You might want to cut back on the coffee a bit."

He chuckled as he slipped a full magazine into the pistol and put it in its shoulder holster. "It's not caffeine. It's anger." He turned to her and continued, "So, what happened?" He'd tasked her with discovering why their attempt to ambush the team at the bunker had failed.

"The trap was good. If we'd been there, we would've gotten them for sure. However, we *weren't* there because the local FBI agent in charge thought he had the situation under control."

Kevin shook his head. "Idiots abound."

The witch nodded. "He decided to roll the dice, hoping

for a number that would mean a promotion. Instead, he gets to report a failure. Of course, he'll figure out a way to make it our fault."

"Naturally." He was silent for a time, thinking through options. "You know, I think this assignment is challenging enough that we're going to need to go out of house. Let me make a call. You can bring the car around."

Ten minutes later, he walked out the front door to find a black SUV waiting for him. It looked like a standard model but was heavily reinforced and capable of high speeds and delivering serious damage to any other participant in a collision.

Tash was behind the wheel. At need, the vehicle could run autonomously, but he generally felt that trusting a car to drive itself was a sucker bet if another option existed. He climbed in and gave her the destination. She asked, "On the books or off?"

"Definitely off."

She opened the armrest and threw her phone inside, and he did the same. They would be out of contact for a while due to the signal-blocking capability of the box they'd put them in, but that was fine. She dialed in the override code to kill the SUV's transponder and trip tracking, then stepped on the gas.

It took an hour to reach the unmarked turnoff to their destination. A long road led between large wooded sections on both sides, the branches above stretching to almost meet above them. They stopped at the heavy metal gate that suddenly appeared as they went around a curve. A guard asked from behind a bulletproof window, "Name?"

"Serrano."

The barrier moved aside, and they drove onto what looked like a small military base. Buildings were clustered together to their left, and a large training area made up the remainder of the cleared space within the circle of trees. They pulled into the parking spot nearest the buildings and climbed out. Tash observed, "Apparently, being a military contractor pays well."

He nodded. "I'm sure it does. Plus, I'm guessing these guys don't turn over everything they find. Kind of like Sheen."

"So, it's okay for them, but not for her?"

"I don't make the rules. And there's a big difference between money and magical artifacts."

She shrugged. "Fair enough."

When they entered the lobby, a man in khakis, an Oxford shirt, and a black sweater atop it shook their hands. Kevin said, "Bradford, good to see you."

"You too, Kev. Let's go into my office to chat." The man's office was easily three times the size of his and filled with everything from sports memorabilia to a World War I era sniper rifle mounted on the wall.

The man across the desk from him had been a sniper in the military, deployed several times. He'd allegedly retired after finishing his twenty but had gone into the private sector doing mostly the same job. Now, he ran one of the most secretive military contracting companies out there. Bradford asked, "So, what do you need?"

Kevin replied, "Support, not sure what kind yet. Ready to move at a moment's notice."

"Targets?"

"Small units. Mixed magicals and not. Highly trained."

Bradford laughed. "So you're the one in charge of the hunt for the people I keep seeing pictures of."

Tash groaned. "Subtle boss, real subtle."

Kevin swiveled his head to glare at his unapologetic second in command. "Shush, you." He turned back to the other man. "Yeah, that's us. We would've had some of them, too, except an overzealous FBI ladder climber decided to try to jump up a few rungs by going solo."

Bradford laughed dismissively. "Heaven save us all from the Bureau. So much righteousness, so little skill."

He felt obliged to chuckle at the other man's comment. "So, give me a number."

He did, and Kevin managed to hide his wince. *That's a lot. Going to have to hit some secret accounts for that.* Fortunately, he'd known such a need might present itself and had arranged for off-the-books access to additional funding. "Done."

Bradford nodded. "Cash. Two weeks upfront, another two in escrow with a mutually selected banker."

"Agreed."

"No magical support on your team?"

He shrugged. "We have a couple, back at the office." He kept Tash's abilities secret wherever possible, believing it gave him an edge in case things went wrong. That belief had been proven valid on several occasions so far, and he held no doubt it would again in the future.

Bradford slapped the desk in exaggerated approval. "Well, let me tell you, you came to the right place. Got a minute? I'd like to show you something."

Kevin confirmed that he did, indeed, have a minute, and the other man led them to a huge building. It was three stories high and reminded him of a football team's indoor practice facility but without the AstroTurf. Weightlifting gear was arranged in one corner, and a few tables and a refrigerator sat nearby. Bradford escorted them to the back of the space and gestured at a group of identically clad people engaged in an incursion scenario.

A small structure was the group's target. He'd seen similar setups in other training facilities, including a few police departments. As they watched, a wizard stepped forward and slashed his wand down, turning the door into shards of wood that flew backward into the facsimile room. The rest of the team moved through the open door, guns at the ready.

Their host sounded proud as he said, "We're still working on full integration of magicals and non-magicals. Most other groups in my line of work keep the two separate, but if you put the magicals under good tactical command, their skills can be really useful."

Kevin felt his subordinate's desire to respond like heat coming off her body and quickly said, "Excellent. We need to run, but I'll have one of my people reach out to set up communication."

Bradford escorted them out to their vehicle and waved farewell as they pulled away. Once they were past the outer gate, Tash finally spoke. "Your friend there is a racist."

Kevin nodded. "No argument from me. I wouldn't call him a friend. More like a useful tool. Emphasis on *tool*."

The witch grunted. "All I can say is, with that attitude, he'd better watch out for friendly fire."

"From the magicals on his team?"

"No. From me."

CHAPTER TWENTY-FIVE

Max was beside himself with excitement, barking up a storm as Rath and Diana fitted his service dog vest around him. He wasn't *really* a service dog, but he did work hard, and they wanted to keep him with them. Diana clipped the lead to his collar and said, "Let's go take a look at this town."

They walked down the shoveled sidewalks of their neighborhood, merging onto the main road after only a few minutes. It was cold and windy, a biting breeze that stung all exposed flesh. For Diana, that was only her face since she'd covered everything else. The heavy winter jacket she wore did nothing for her figure, but it kept her warm, which was all she cared about. It also hid the pistol in her shoulder holster.

The face others would see wasn't hers. She was maintaining an illusion for herself and Rath, who simply appeared to be a child. He, too, was wrapped in heavy boots and an insulated puffy jacket that looked hilarious on him. She carefully didn't laugh or mention that to him, though, simply enjoyed the sight. He and Max chased each other through the deep snow, and the troll threw snowballs while the dog tried biting them out of the air.

Diana grinned at their antics, her spirits lifting into their normal range for only the second time since they'd left the base, the first being the movie marathon with Rath after confirming her people were all okay. He'd chosen comedies instead of action films, and they'd laughed until breathing was a challenge. *Maybe this won't be such a bad place to spend the winter.* Scenario Zulu had no specific duration, only a series of checkpoints they had to reach before they could bring the team back together.

The initial one of those had already gone awry. She'd found an email waiting in a rarely used account with the codewords that said Cara and Hank were safe, but their enemy had compromised their secondary base. Remembering that sobered her a little. *Whoever's after us is good at what they do. Bastards.*

They reached the grocery, which was about the size of a convenience store in most of the places she'd lived. She stopped and pointed at her companions. "You two behave. Especially you, Max. But *especially* you, Rath." The troll giggled, and she opened the door, passing through under the chiming bell that announced an entry. She grabbed a basket and moved down the aisles, filling it with easy meals.

Diana could cook, was pretty good at it, in fact, but didn't have the mental energy to devote to it right now. So it would be pasta with jarred sauce and some additional spices, sandwiches, omelets, and a lot of toast and jam for the near term. As they looped around to the next row and walked back toward the front, she couldn't help but over-hear a woman talking to the cashier.

The voice was a little thready, definitely not young, and held a tone she categorized immediately as gossip. She smothered a smile at the thought that every small town was awash in conversation and speculation about the neighbors.

They looped around the end at the front of the store, and she got a look at the woman. Sure enough, she had short white hair and thick glasses, but the way she held herself spoke of frequent exercise, something she'd noticed most New Englanders shared, even more so on the Cape. *Lots of hiking, lots of winter sports, plus swimming. Makes sense.* Diana's attention was caught by the woman saying, "I've never seen anything like it. Anthony hasn't been himself at all. Do you know, he beat up his next-door neighbor?"

Diana stopped and made a show of looking through the contents of the shelves while listening carefully to the woman's words as they spilled out of her. "I mean, that man had always been a pain. Not taking care of his prop-erty, scowling at everyone who walked by. But Anthony? I would have sworn he'd never hurt a fly. Nicest gent I ever knew. Well, not anymore."

The woman changed topics as the cashier finished ringing her up, and Diana walked with purpose through the rest of the aisle and up the next, loading up her basket quickly. Rath tuned into her attitude because he and Max came along quietly, not distracting her. The woman was out on the street by the time they were at the cash register.

As the cashier rang them up, Diana asked, "Who was that? I think I've seen her around, but I'm not sure."

"Oh, that's Mrs. Victor. Her husband died a few years ago. She lives a ways over there." The woman gestured in the direction of Diana's current residence. "Don't think I've seen you in here before."

Diana smiled. "Just staying in town for a few days, on the way up to Provincetown. We rented a house there. Going to do some painting."

"Oh, you're an artist? Have I seen your work?"

She laughed. "Not yet. You will, though. Keep an eye out for seascapes from P-town. That'll be the name of the series. I hope to put it in galleries all over the Cape next summer, maybe catch some tourist cash."

The cashier nodded. "Sounds like a good plan. I'll be sure to remember."

Diana took the paper bags, one in each arm, and headed out. Rath held onto Max's leash as she strode quickly forward, wanting to close the distance with the older woman. Her quarry turned into a café a couple of blocks away. Diana said, "When we get there, you and Max stay outside with the groceries. I'm going to go in for a cup of coffee and some gossip."

Rath replied, "And hot chocolate. And a bowl of whipped cream for Max."

She laughed. "You drive a hard bargain, buddy. Sure."

The troll added, "So cold here."

"It is. I'd forgotten how wicked the winters are. Still, it's a good hiding spot, probably. Assuming that woman believes the story I made up. Guess I better order some art supplies, just in case."

He cocked his head to the side. "Does Amazon even deliver up here in the winter?"

She shrugged. "Probably. If not, I'm sure Andercarr does. They're everywhere."

She left the pair outside and walked in, taking her place in line at the ordering counter. The older woman's voice was loud enough to carry from where she waited for her drink and talked to the barista. She was saying, "It's just not like Anthony to behave that way. Scared his wife so much, she went to her sister's. Now he's all alone in the house. I have no idea what's going on. And apparently, he must've hurt himself."

The man making her coffee drink dutifully asked, "Why do you say that?"

The gossip replied, "I saw him stomping through his yard, kind of waving his arms and muttering. He wore a t-shirt and no coat, which was crazy, given how cold it was. Bandages wrapped his right arm from the wrist up to the elbow. I don't know what he could've done to hurt himself that much, but I'm sure it couldn't have been fun." Her tone changed from remembrance to anticipation. "Anyway, the neighbor is still in the hospital, but I imagine he's going to be upset when he gets out. Didn't press charges, though, which is weird."

The conversation turned to other matters, but the woman's words bounced around her mind. Each time they rebounded from one of her mental walls, her level of concern rose that much higher. The woman left before Diana got her drinks, but she wasn't in a rush anymore. She'd gotten all she needed from the stranger and a lot more than she wanted.

She walked outside and handed Rath his hot chocolate, and they both sipped from their paper cups while Max lapped up his whipped cream. The troll asked, "Get anything?"

She replied, "Too much. I'll tell you when we're closer to home."

Once Max was done, they set out for home, Diana awkwardly juggling the two bags of groceries while trying not to spill her coffee. When she was sure they were alone, she said, "Okay, here's what I heard." She shared the information he hadn't been present for. When she finished, she lowered her voice. "Bandaged arm. You know what that could mean."

Rath's tone was uncommonly solemn. "An artifact?"

Diana nodded. "That's what I think. It would explain the personality change, possibly. Especially since it went in a violent direction when the person had no history of it."

"We're going to check it out." It was a statement, not a question.

"Yeah, we are. As carefully as possible. Fortunately, tonight's supposed to be cloudy, so there won't be much moonlight. I guess it's time to test out those wings, buddy."

CHAPTER TWENTY-SIX

The ascent to a good launch point had been a difficult one. The highest spot in the area was the top of the church steeple. The climb had been slow going because of the snow that had collected on the roof and the ice that coated the spire. Still, Rath was a determined troll and made it up there safely.

He wore layers of shirts and thin jackets, the winter one he'd been using too bulky for his harness. It was cold, the wind up here biting into his flesh and ruffling his hair, which probably had ice crystals in it by now. Rath laughed. "I'm a trollcicle."

Diana, who had a matching cell phone with an open call to his, replied, "Be careful. Remember, you don't have your grapnel."

There were a *lot* of things Rath didn't have. He didn't have his safety device, he didn't have his best knives, he didn't have the new, better version of his wings, and he didn't have a guarantee that these would open, even though they'd done so on his ground-level tests. He *did* have his batons and an older version of Gwen in the goggles that had been with his backup gear. He'd agreed with Diana's concern that the new version in his glasses might not be as well-suited for this adventure.

He set his feet on the side of the steeple and gripped the base of the pole atop it with both hands. "Gwen, mark the house, please." They'd programmed the address in before he started his climb. An area in his display glowed. He shifted his position to get the best angle toward it. "Okay, got it. Air currents, please."

A visual map of the local airflow appeared. It was less complete and detailed than he was used to because the goggles only had their sensors to work with. Normally, they would be able to access the base computers, which had a connection to all sorts of things, including weather radar. Still, it was enough that he could see where he could avoid losing altitude more rapidly than other spots. "Okay. Troll flight one, good to go."

Diana chuckled, and he pictured her shaking her head. He liked making her laugh and considered it a life goal to do it as often as possible. She said, "Remember, one pass over for recon, then land safely. If it looks clean, I'll be nearby by the time you're ready to go in. If it doesn't, we meet up at the rendezvous point."

"Affirmative, yep, you got it, totally tubular. Banzai." He launched himself from the spire, slapping the button on his chest where the harness straps met to extend his wings. They snapped out exactly as intended and caught the air, turning his fall into a glide. He banked slightly to stay on course. "Magnify, please." The image in his goggles grew larger, and he trained them on the house with the man who was acting strangely.

A path overlaid his vision, and he followed it, automatically curving and dipping where Gwen told him to, the act of flying with the AI familiar enough that he didn't have to concentrate on it nearly as much as he had in the beginning. "Lights on the second floor. Seems to be shades. I can't see inside. No lights on the first floor." He frowned at a sound that had come from somewhere. "Gwen, increase audio, please."

The speakers pointed at his ears grew louder, and he heard yelling and the sound of crashing. When he turned his head, and the goggles' microphones swiveled away from the house, the sounds lessened. When he moved it back, they increased. "Sounds like he's breaking furniture or something."

Diana growled, "More evidence that it might be an artifact. Dammit. Do you see anything worth calling this off over?"

He gave the whole area another once over and replied, "Nope."

"Okay. Put down, and I'll meet you at the back of the house in ten minutes." A timer appeared in the corner of his vision, counting down.

"Got it. Troll flight one, heading in for a landing."

Rath descended in a wide spiral and touched down a block away in a kids' playground. He retracted the wings and ran for the house, wanting to get there before Diana did as one more point in his favor in their ongoing competition. He'd lost several board games after the movie marathon, so he needed to pick up some points.

The fact that Diana wasn't aware reaching the house first was a way to earn them didn't matter at all. He'd tell her once she arrived. *After me, of course.*

Diana stayed close to the house to avoid their target seeing her from the second-story windows, presumably where he was. Her glasses had picked out Rath's heat signature, and she watched him cross the space from the tree he was hiding behind to her position in a low crouch. Upon arrival, he whispered, "I was here first. Point to me."

Diana sighed. He was forever inventing competitions she knew nothing about. "Fair enough. We ready?"

He drew his batons from their sheaths. They'd had no way to recharge them fully. Hank and Anik had been able to get his induction gloves out of the armory, but the battery pack hadn't come along. Diana had managed to rig a charger, so each baton had about one charge worth of stun capability.

She'd carried a document tube over her shoulder, and now she set it down, pulling a sheathed Fury out of it. A pistol rested under her coat, but using it would be problematic since silencers weren't part of their tactical gear. Her boots held throwing knives and stilettos.

She was deeply uncomfortable with the current situation. Finding an artifact in their figurative backyard seemed coincidental, but for all she knew, an enemy could be tracking them. She believed the Remembrance, the gang they'd put out of business in Pittsburgh, was truly gone since she'd dispatched its leadership. *Really, who knows?*

There could be more, and they might be involved in what's going on. I doubt it. She felt her mind starting to go in circles. *I need to quit being so paranoid.*

Diana used telekinesis to unlock the back door, and they walked into a small mudroom. The floor creaked underneath them, and she pointed at it. Rath nodded and took the lead, moving a few feet in front of her. They cleared the first level, walking through a small kitchen, dining room, and living room. Space was at a premium on the Cape, so the houses tended to be on the modest side. She expected the upstairs would be one bedroom and a bathroom, or at most two rooms.

They reached the bottom of the stairs, and she reviewed them carefully, looking for traps as her glasses flicked through detection modes. The heat sensing function displayed a figure on the top floor, stomping around and making the boards creak, which was likely why their passage had gone unnoticed despite the old hardwood. Rath climbed the staircase slowly at a gesture from her. She followed a step behind, holding Fury by the scabbard in her left hand with the hilt facing slightly upward, ready for a draw. She hoped not to have to cut the man's arm off and prayed she wouldn't have to kill him.

The top of the stairs ended with a turn and an open door. The man walked past as they reached it, and he screamed at the sight of Rath. It wasn't fear. It was unbridled fury. The troll dashed forward under his grasping arms, clearing the way for Diana to gain the upper level. She threw a bolt of force at the man, but tentacles erupted out of his arm, weaving themselves into a shield to intercept her magical attack.

With a frustrated sigh, she jerked the sheath forward and caught Fury as it slid out. She dropped the sheath and rushed ahead, swinging at the tentacles. The man moved quicker than she would've thought possible given his bulk, dodging strikes from Rath's baton.

The tendrils seemed to be fighting separately from him, and they darted faster than any she'd ever seen, trying to rip Fury from her grasp as she swiped and slashed at them. Several snuck in at her feet, and she dragged the point along the wooden floor, separating them from their source as they wrapped around her ankles.

The man howled, a crazed sound, almost inhuman. *I wonder if this is what it looks like when an artifact takes over completely. Terrifying.*

She threw more force blasts, knocking the tentacles out of the way as they sought her neck, and snapped out a line of force to snag one that was going for Rath. The troll snuck in a blow, striking the man in the leg. His stun baton *snapped* loudly, and their foe's body went momentarily rigid. The tentacles, though, weren't affected, and they whipped out at Diana and forced her to put most of her effort into defense.

The fight was loud, and she didn't want the neighbors or local police to get involved. She murmured the command word to activate the shield charm in her bracelet. The tiny metal piece burned away, but the tentacles could no longer reach her. She ran forward and slammed into the crazed man, who was now literally frothing at the mouth, and knocked him off balance. Rath's other baton stabbed him in the chest, and this time their opponent went down.

Diana quickly searched the man's broken dresser, finding clothes to use to tie him up. She and Rath bound his body from ankle to neck in pieces of clothing. She had no idea what the tentacles might be capable of once he regained consciousness, but she was fairly sure they wouldn't be able to untie knots. *Hopefully.* She looked at Rath. "We'd better find some rope."

The troll nodded. "Thinking the same thing." They found some in the kitchen and used it to bind him further until Diana felt they'd done all they could. Her partner asked, "Now what?"

She sighed. "Well, we can't take him with us, so we need to have someone come get him."

"Not local police."

Diana shook her head. "No." She pulled out her prepaid phone and dialed the number she'd gotten from Ruby in Magic City but had hoped never to have to use. *I didn't expect I'd have to use it after our involvement in Ely was over.*

She pressed Send, and a moment later, Director of the Boston Paranormal Defense Agency bureau Paul Andrews said, "Who is this? How did you get this number?"

Diana replied, "Someone on the same side of things as you are. You need to detail a recovery team to the location I'm about to give you. A Rhazdon artifact has infected a local. He seems rather insane." She gave the address.

He demanded, "Who is this? Why should I listen to you?"

"We have an acquaintance in common. I don't think you'd call her a friend, though. Wears a mask."

He groaned. "Okay. Team's on the way. Now you tell me who you are."

Instead of doing so, she crossed into the nearby bathroom, dropped the phone in the tub, and used fire to destroy it. Rath threw his in beside hers. They headed outside, and Diana said, "Well, there goes our idyllic winter on the Cape. Let's go get Max and head to our secondary location." She opened a portal back to their small house.

As they stepped through, Rath said, "I wanted to ski."

"Me too, buddy. There's probably skiing in Seattle, assuming we can safely leave the house."

As she closed the rift behind them, she said, "I wonder how many of these damn artifacts are out there. Not being sold on the black market or used by magicals with malicious intent, just infecting regular people and creating chaos?"

He shrugged. "No way to tell. I hope the PDA can help him."

Diana nodded. "Agreed. I think we might have found a new secondary mission for our team. Ordinary people who get mixed up with these damn things need the kind of help we're uniquely suited to offer."

CHAPTER TWENTY-SEVEN

It didn't take them long to pack up since they'd never really unpacked, and the cross-country trip was accomplished in only an instant as they stepped from their house in Cape Cod to the top floor of a house in Seattle. Originally a single-family home, rising prices and the booming housing market had forced the woman on the first floor to convert the second to an apartment.

Through a series of cutouts, Diana had been renting the upper floor for almost six months. She'd put in an appearance now and again, always in disguise, explaining that she was a frequent traveler who was often overseas and needed a place she could call home from time to time. The woman had said she understood, and Diana got the impression that home meant a lot to her.

It was only four rooms: a bedroom, main room, kitchen, and a bathroom. She sighed, having preferred their last hideout a great deal more than this. *Well, there could be skiing, right?*

Her inner voice replied, "Good plan. Maybe you can get nabbed by the FBI while enjoying your winter sports."

She didn't even have the energy to tell her inner critic to shut up. Besides, it was correct. In the current situation, the only way they could go out in public was in disguise, and she wasn't the best at maintaining disguises for herself and Rath while doing other complicated things. *Especially not hurtling down the side of a mountain on a pair of sticks.*

She found herself pacing, with Rath in the middle of the room watching her, a concerned expression growing on his face. She forced herself to stop moving, drew a deep breath, and blew it deliberately out. "Okay. New place. I grabbed enough food for tonight, so we're clear there."

The troll nodded. "Maybe a bath?"

Diana smothered a reflexive frown. She had, on occasion, used long baths and showers to relax, so it wasn't a terrible idea. She was still too keyed up right now, too focused on work, to find contentment that way. "Good thought, buddy, but I think I need something else. You two stay in here, watch some TV. I'm going to have a chat with Fury."

Rath smiled and hugged the Borzoi, who had been lying next to him watching her pace. "Tell him I said hi."

Diana chuckled. "Will do, buddy." She went into the bedroom and closed the door, bringing only her sheathed sword with her. Sitting on the bed, she swung her legs up, crossed them, and arranged herself properly, back straight and weight centered. She pulled the sword from the sheath and set the latter aside, placing the weapon across her lap. Her left hand descended to rest lightly on the blade near the point, and her right did the same on the hilt. She closed her eyes and sent her thoughts inward.

The sentient being inside the sword was as eager to speak with her as she was with him. It took only an instant for the trappings of the sword's interior world to surround her. It was Japan-inspired, shoji panels making walls on all sides, a wooden floor polished so well it almost glowed connected to similarly treated wooden posts climbing upward to crossbeams on the ceiling.

Tapestries and banners inscribed with calligraphy hung in several places. She was seated on a cushion in front of a black lacquer table. A traditional tea service rested on its surface. Opposite her was the avatar of the being inside the sword. He was all sharp edges, his cheekbones, his eyes, his eyebrows, and thin lips. He wore his traditional sword-fighting outfit, a red tunic and long black skirt. His deep voice, harsh with its Japanese accent, nonetheless conveyed warmth. "Diana. Welcome." He inclined his head in a small bow.

She matched it. "*Arigato*. It's been a while."

He nodded sharply. "Perhaps, in the future, it might not be so."

It was criticism but delivered with enough nuance she could choose not to take it as such. Instead, she owned it. "Yeah, I know. The fact that I've been busy is no excuse."

"As you say." He leaned forward and busied himself with preparing the tea. "What has brought you here today?"

She sighed, keeping her eyes on his hands as he did the same. Sometimes, it was easier to be truthful when one didn't look their conversational partner in the face. "I'm uncharacteristically unmoored at the moment. I've been in this place before, but only transitionally. I feel a little stuck right now, to be honest."

His head dipped in a nod. "So, you retreat to that which you know best, seeking solid ground. This is wise."

"It's kind of you to say so."

He glanced upward with a small smile. "Rest assured, wielder. I'll never tell you anything other than the truth. I am incapable of flattery."

A grin twitched at the edges of her mouth. "So you say. I'm not sure I believe it."

One side of his lips quirked. "Again, it is wisdom not to trust blindly."

She laughed. "Talking with you is like stretching out my brain and tying it in random knots."

"That would be something to see, indeed." His dry delivery, signaling humor, changed to a more serious one. "So. Tell me about the situation that vexes you so."

The preparations completed, he handed her a cup and lifted his. Together, they inhaled the scents of the complex green tea, then sipped in silence, savoring the experience. When the ritual had done its work of calming her mind, she set the cup down carefully on the tray.

"My team and I are on the run from an opponent with more resources. He's claimed our base and is enlisting the public against us. We've gone from being in a superior position to an inferior one with the revelation of this new enemy."

He nodded. "Do you expect an open confrontation? Or will the game of fox and hare continue?"

"The latter, most likely." As she said the words, that

knowledge clicked into place in a way it hadn't before. She'd been thinking down old paths, which were unproductive in their new reality. *This isn't one of our usual straight-up fights. I need to quit treating it like it is.*

Fury was silent while she marshaled her thoughts. When she looked up, he advised, "The wisest course is to prepare the field of battle, whatever it may be, to your best advantage *and* allow your enemy to know you are doing so. Then, when they believe they have a clear picture of your intentions, attack where your foe least expects it."

Diana considered the sword's words. *They wouldn't expect us to go after the Serrano guy in Washington. That would come as a big shock indeed.* Out loud, she asked, "So, cut the head off the snake?"

He shrugged, which was usually a signal she'd said something he disagreed with. "Most leaders expect that the fight will come to them. That might not be the *least* predictable course, although they would certainly expect it less than a direct conflict between armies."

"You've given me a lot to think about." Whatever her brain might've decided to say next vanished as her magical sixth sense warned her of hostile magic. She snapped back out of the virtual space and into her physical one, hurling herself off the bed with one hand and raising Fury to strike with the other.

A portal finished opening in the back corner of the bedroom, and through it, she saw something she didn't expect—Bryant, with an unfamiliar room behind him. He took a step into the bedroom, and Diana moved forward into his embrace. She rested her head on his chest and scolded, "You're an idiot. You shouldn't be here. It's not safe."

He rubbed his cheek against her hair. "I know. I couldn't handle being apart right now."

"I'm glad you came."

He drew a deep breath and let it out in a sigh. The portal shrank to nothingness behind him as he released the magic. "Me too."

After a few minutes of simply standing together, they headed out into the main room. Max almost wagged his body in a full circle, led by his tail, in his excitement to see Bryant. Her boyfriend sat on the floor and accepted the dog's enthusiastic licks while Rath laughed and laughed. When everyone had settled down, Diana said, "I feel aimless. I have no idea where to go or what to do because we don't have any information."

The troll paused his game, which was flipping one of his knives in the air and catching it by the blade with his fingertips. "I think this is all too big for only us. Even now that Bryant's here."

Diana frowned. "Zulu's conditions for gathering in person haven't been met. Our next virtual get-together is a couple of days away."

Bryant spoke softly and calmly. "Maybe it's time to improvise."

Rath crowed, "Bryant votes to improvise. I vote to improvise. Max votes to improvise. You know what that means? It's time to improvise."

Diana couldn't help laughing. She shook her head and pointed at Rath. "You are trouble." She moved the finger to Bryant. "You, doubly so." Finally, she pointed at the dog.

"You too, disloyal mutt. Remember, I was your friend before you ever met these guys."

The Borzoi came over and climbed into her lap, dropping his weight on her with a *thump* and sticking his head back against her chest, his tongue trying to reach far enough to lick her face.

Diana laughed along with the others, running her fingers through his fur. "Okay. To hell with continuing Zulu. It's time we started thinking differently."

CHAPTER TWENTY-EIGHT

Deacon cruised through the magical dark web, reveling in the freedom he felt in that particular virtual place. For him, it looked a lot like something from the second *Tron* film, a landscape of wireframe objects, pulsing connections, and an overwhelming sense that one was swimming in a maelstrom of data begging for him to tap into it.

Of course, randomly trying to access any of the things around him could result in all sorts of bad outcomes. This was where the most virulent viruses, the most wicked weapons, and the most hazardous programs lived. He was in his element, but doubtless, most of the other info-mancers with him in the space felt the same. *They probably all think they're the best, too, like I do. Occupational hazard, I guess.*

As he flew through the virtual realm, bright lights scattered out of his path, bots and programs from other users unwilling to risk offending him. He frowned as his instincts warned him that some of them seemed not to be randomly fleeing but were deliberately moving in a common direction. He waved to summon a spell, which in the real world activated programs on his computer system and put them to work.

Walls materialized to capture one of the glowing dots, trapping it in a cube. He moved seamlessly through the transparent wall and grabbed the bot, pulling it apart with his bare hands. Glitter exploded out of it, bright red and sparkling, to form a web address. Alongside it was a single word, "Jewel." He muttered, "Holy hell," in both the virtual and physical worlds.

His reflexive response to being poked was to call up programs to bounce his signal across the world, a more aggressive series of hops than the standard paths he used that only went through twenty-seven. The new routing would increase his lag, but he didn't anticipate a fight ahead. *Hopefully.*

When his rerouting was complete, he marshaled his offensive and defensive programs, had his system send a text message to Kayleigh explaining what was going on, and before he could think better of it, he sent himself to the address the bot had held. The sensation of fast movement filled the next several seconds, which in virtual space was a notably long interval.

He landed in a featureless white room. Taking a step forward resulted in no change, and he suspected the walls, if walls there were, would move away from him as he advanced, so he never reached them.

He wasn't trapped since he could always log out if simply trying to command himself to a new location failed. Still, he'd come here by invitation, so he didn't feel the need to leave quite yet. An avatar shimmered into being, one he recognized as someone he knew, even though they'd never met in person. "Demetrius?"

The other man nodded. His virtual representation was a cartoon Rastafarian, complete with the hat. "Yeah. Ruby is using me to do her crap work, as usual." They laughed together.

Deacon said, "What's up?"

"She wants to meet with Diana. Says it's important."

"What about?"

Demetrius chuckled, and his avatar lifted its arms and dropped them helplessly. "Please. Like she tells me anything. It probably has something to do with the fact that your team's names and pictures are plastered all over the Internet."

Deacon scratched the back of his neck. "Yeah, we're not exactly low-profile at the moment, true."

"So, can you set up a meet?"

"If the boss agrees, sure. Give me a place to contact you."

A familiar sense of excitement surged inside Kayleigh for the first time since they'd left the base. She wasn't a believer in fate or anything. Still, when Ruby's request coincided with a message from Diana calling for an unscheduled get-together, it seemed too perfect to be completely coincidental. The sudden and entirely unexpected "on the right path" vibe that filled her made her almost giddy with anticipation.

She and Deacon repeated the process of readying the meeting room. Then she launched it. The team assembled within a minute. A couple of minutes later, she was able to set aside her worry about their safety. Everyone had reported being in a stable location, safe and sound.

Diana changed the subject, announcing, "We're officially abandoning scenario Zulu. It kept us safe when bad things happened, which is what it was supposed to do. Now that we all have our sea legs, so to speak, it's time we started thinking forward, rather than thinking backward."

Hank grumbled, "That's a lot of thinking, boss. I'm not sure Cara's up to it."

Everyone laughed, and the target of his insult replied, "Screw you, meathead."

Kayleigh reluctantly abandoned the entertaining crosstalk and created a channel with only Diana. "We have a guest at the door. Your friend from Magic City would like to chat with us. Okay with you?"

Diana asked, "You have all the security issues locked down?"

Deacon gave her a disgusted look over the table, and Kayleigh answered dryly, "Deacon says yes, everything's fine, thank you for asking."

Diana chuckled. "I'm sure those were his exact words. Yeah, let her in."

Ruby's greeting set off a couple of minutes of chatter, people asking how she was, what was going on, followed by their guest returning the same questions to them.

Finally, once that wrapped up, Ruby said, "I thought you might need a temporary base of operations. It just so happens

I have a lovely underground bunker. It'll be a bit of a tight fit, depending on how much stuff you have since the builder constructed it in a time when living space expectations were a little less optimistic than they are now. You're welcome to every inch of it, as long as you don't mind sharing with us."

Kayleigh was surprised to find more hope surging through her, something she wouldn't have thought possible at the start of the meeting. Time seemed to freeze while she and the others waited for Diana's answer, which would drastically affect at least their near-term futures. Finally, the boss said, "That's an amazing offer. We'll owe you big. We accept, and thank you." Cheers greeted her words, followed by laughter as everyone realized they all shared the same feelings.

Ruby sounded entirely pleased. "Don't worry. I'll come up with a reasonable payback system. I think each member of your team should act as my servant on a rotating basis." More laughter mixed with friendly insults drowned out her words.

Diana said, "Okay, folks. Play time's over. Let's figure out the best way to make this happen."

A half-hour later, the meeting ended, and Kayleigh circled the table to hug Deacon from behind. She rested her chin on his shoulder. "Thank the universe for that. I can't wait."

He reached up to hold her arms. "Me neither."

She sniffed a little. "This has been hard."

His voice held a note of suspicion as he confirmed, "Yeah, it has."

She delivered the killing blow with a wide grin. "Being

217

stuck with you, I mean. *Damn*, it'll be awesome to be around normal people again."

He made a sound between a sigh and a choked laugh. "Bite me, Kitana. You suck."

Kayleigh spun away with a laugh. "We'd better get packing. Things will move fast from here."

CHAPTER TWENTY-NINE

F iguring out spots where Diana could meet her people, then portal them to Ruby in a safe location, who then portaled them to the bunker, had been a logistical challenge. Adding in the amount of gear they had to move, which in some cases was plentiful, made it an even bigger hassle. Hank had whined about having to leave his van behind as soon as they'd joined her, but Cara had rolled her eyes dramatically and told him to shut up. Diana figured a story was involved, probably an entertaining one, but it wasn't the right moment to find out.

The bunker was something out of the fifties. Ruby explained it had been a rich person's idea of a bomb shelter and that a friend had essentially rented it out to her and her team for as long as they needed to use it. Amid the hustle and bustle of getting things into the place and finding an arrangement that would suit their needs while minimally impacting their hosts, Diana asked Ruby, "So, what's it like, being in charge of an entire group of magicals?"

The other woman gave a small laugh. "Every step of the way along the path to becoming *Mirra* of the Mist Elves, I thought, 'This is crazy. I can't do this.' Now I have confirmation that I was right."

Diana laughed, and Idryll, Ruby's magical companion, adopted a long-suffering expression. "She's not really this humble. It's an act. She's a *tyrant*, I tell you. Take it from someone who has to spend far, far too much time with her."

At Diana's side, Rath giggled. "That sounds familiar."

She replied, "Shut it. Go play with Max. Leave me alone. Forever." The troll scampered off, his laughter unabated.

Ruby turned to her companion. "See? That's how this relationship is supposed to work. You go away now."

The shapeshifter, with her striking orange, gold, and black hair that matched her tiger-form colorings, stared disdainfully at Ruby for a second, then wandered off without replying. The other woman sighed. "I'll pay for that, eventually. Probably with something involving claws. That's not important right now. Anything I can do for you at the moment?"

Diana shook her head. "You've set us up perfectly, thanks."

Ruby nodded. "Okay. I have a couple of errands to run, but I'll be back in a while." She crossed into what she called the receiving room, a small chamber that had been their exclusive portal in, and now portal out, point. *Wonder if it's the only place that it works or something.* That thought sparked another, then another, and the faint glimmer of an idea started to build in her mind.

She turned and scanned the crowd, spotting Deacon and Kayleigh setting up computer equipment through the open doorway to the small storeroom. She walked over and tapped them on the shoulders. "Come with me." She led them into Ruby's workshop, cautioning, "Touch nothing. Close the door."

They complied, and Deacon asked, "What's up, boss?"

Diana stared at them both for a second, but they returned blank looks. *Which proves they know why I've called them in here,* "Time to tell the truth."

Kayleigh replied quickly, "About what?" That was all the confirmation Diana needed to be positive the tech was hiding a secret. They'd lived and worked together for long enough that some things were almost guaranteed. *Like the fact that these two couldn't follow a set of orders if their lives depended on it. Literally.*

She shook her head. "I know you didn't kill everything back at the base. You wouldn't have. Not in your nature. Even with Clean Slate activated, I bet you had to do *something* that broke the rules. Now spill. What was it?"

The pair looked at one another and exchanged sighs. Deacon sounded slightly embarrassed as he said, "I have a couple of bots around. Small ones but high-functioning. I always considered it a *backup* to the backup plan. They look exactly like the skin of the vimana, so there's no way anyone will notice they're different from any other part of the walls' designs. Believe me. I threw every scan I had at them. When they're inert, they're undetectable."

"What about when they're not?"

He shrugged. "A little electrical spillage, plus someone

might see them moving. They're small enough that most motion detectors won't, though."

She shook her head. "Not what I'm asking. What can they do?"

"Little bots for little things. They have a cutting blade, a computer interface, and the ability to use an appendage to press buttons. That's about it."

Diana nodded. "Okay, that's part of the picture. What's the rest of it, Kayleigh?"

The tech put her hands on her hips. "You immediately assume I'm involved. Why, because we're dating?"

She shook her head. "No, because you're *you*. Not the time for games. Tell me."

Kayleigh smiled. "Well, to make the bots work, you have to be able to communicate with them. So, I took out the part of Zulu and Clean Slate where the secondary communication system gets fragged."

"Is it working?"

"It should be, but I truly haven't had an opportunity to check. Since we're trying to keep our presence hidden, I didn't think it was a good idea, anyway."

"Makes sense. Is there a way you can verify it without giving us away?"

The tech nodded. "The system uploads its status to the base computer systems daily, but when it can't reach them, it uses a satellite once a week as a secondary report. That procedure is essentially there for situations like this, to confirm it's operational and in contact. All we have to do is log in to the satellite's communication buffer and see if it checked in."

Positive energy was building inside Diana, a welcome

feeling given how little of it she'd felt since leaving the base. "Well, hell. Go check, woman."

After getting a better understanding from Deacon about what his bots could do, and after Kayleigh had verified the backup comm system was still operational, Diana walked to the center of the main room and clapped sharply. "Okay, people, listen up. I have a plan. It's something our enemies definitely won't see coming."

Conversations died as everyone turned to face her. Cara said, "Don't keep us waiting, Boss."

She smiled. Certainty about the path ahead filled her. "We're going to break back into our base, grab intel, snag some artifacts, and maybe even get some of the gear we left behind."

Silence reigned for several moments until Tony smoothed his mustache and asked, "Are we doing this because it's strategically smart, or are we doing it because we want to give the assholes who took our home some payback?"

Her smile turned into a full grin. "Both. For one more reason, as well. They think they have us on the run. They think we're scared, wringing our hands with anxiety over our imminent capture, prosecution, and hell, who knows, maybe execution."

That was laying on a little thick, but she was in a groove. "Here's the thing. We're going to show them they don't scare us a bit by going back to the place where they hit us and punching them in the mouth so hard they'll be trying to find the splinters of their teeth for days."

Smiles blossomed on every face. Rath yelled, "I'm in, so *very* in."

Each member of the team confirmed that they were, too, and Diana felt a familiar pride in her peoples' spirit. She said, "We're still going to try to remain nonlethal, so plan accordingly. The rest of us will take six hours to rest while Kayleigh and Deacon get some prep done. Sleep if you can. After that, though, we gear up and show these people exactly how big a mistake they made in choosing to mess with us."

———

Diana permitted herself a beer as she sat on the couch in the main room. Cara, in a chair beside it, also held a can of a local craft brew in her hand. She wasn't paying attention to anything other than her conversation with Cara and was spending a good portion of the non-drink-sipping time with her eyes closed and her head tilted back. It surprised her when Ruby's voice came from nearby. "Hey, you two, can I chat with you for a minute in my workshop?"

Diana blinked the gumminess out of her eyes, exchanged looks with her second-in-command, then rose. "Of course." Cara was a step behind as they followed their host into the other room. Waiting inside was the completely unexpected figure of Nylotte, Diana's mentor, and lately, Cara's teacher as well. Diana couldn't restrain herself from going forward and wrapping the other woman in a hug.

The Drow patted her back with a laugh. "It's lovely to see you too, Diana. You too, Cara."

Diana stepped back and stared at her teacher. The dark elf had always possessed a certain martial aspect, but now it was more pronounced. She wore black leather armor, and the hilt of a sword stuck up over her shoulder. She'd tied her white hair in a warrior's topknot, its substantial length spilling down her back in a ponytail bound by a series of leather ties. She said, "You look like you're about to go to war with someone."

Nylotte smiled. "The version of me you're most familiar with is only one of many, my student. This is another. I've taken it upon myself to do a little of the work your team normally handles, seeking out magical artifacts and taking them away from people who would misuse them."

Cara asked, "Are you planning to join us, then?"

The Drow shook her head. "No. I only stopped by to let you know that I'm here for you. You can get in touch with me through Ruby whenever, and I can always find my way to Diana at need."

She said, "Really?"

A short laugh escaped the other woman. "There is much about magic that you have yet to understand, Diana. Of course, I know where you and Cara are at all times. I'm attuned to you because we have worked so closely together."

She frowned. "That seems like it would get annoying if you had a lot of students."

Nylotte nodded. "Which is why I select so few."

"Any advice?"

Her mentor laughed. "Now that you're beyond the inevitable sulking you've doubtless been engaged in? None. Be yourselves. Trust your powers. You are adequate to any task, as long as you don't let your brains get in the way."

The other woman had said words to that effect before, but a reminder was always good.

Cara asked, "Are you sure you won't come along? We're going to take the fight to our enemies, finally."

"No. But I am a resource and a refuge if you need it. Even if the entire world knows you're with me, still, you shall remain safe. Worst case, I'll spirit you away to the deep woods on Oriceran, and we'll plan our vengeance from there."

Diana and Cara both nodded. Her second-in-command said, "Thank you."

She echoed her appreciation and added, "I feared it would be much longer before we would be together again."

Nylotte laughed and stood fully from where she'd been seated on the edge of the table. "As if I'd let such a thing happen. Now, go do your work. You both need to get back to your regular training sessions as soon as possible before you lose all the skills I've taught you."

CHAPTER THIRTY

With a plan in hand, Diana's team focused on gearing up. Ruby had supplied all the equipment she could, including electrical grenades, gas grenades, and flash-bangs. The need to try to stay nonlethal, especially when magic would be sporadically useful at best because of the anti-magic emitters, upped the op's degree of difficulty considerably.

Diana took a moment to check out her people scattered around the bunker's main room. Some had their normal vests. Some wore only armor that Ruby had borrowed, off the books, from Sheriff Alejo. Pistols were present, and some rifles as well, but they wouldn't get used except as a last resort.

Kayleigh had made it out with enough prototype web grenades that each team could have two, but the tech hadn't guaranteed their functionality. "There's a reason they're only prototypes, you see. If you all understood any sort of science, that would be clear." The comment had earned her nothing but mockery, which Diana felt had been well-deserved.

Satisfied with her people's preparations, she went into one of the bunker's storerooms. Kayleigh and Deacon had chosen that spot for their setup because it offered the best network access. She said, "The team will finish prepping in a few minutes. Time for you to do your thing."

The two sat back-to-back, each staring into their computer monitor. Kayleigh asked, "Ready?"

Deacon replied, "Waiting on you, now."

The blonde shook her head. "Moron. Okay, sending the activation signal to the backup system." After a long second, she continued, "Link established. It's booting out of standby mode."

The tech's eyes stayed glued to the screen, which meant she couldn't see the exasperated look on Diana's face. Sometimes, the technical aspects of a job seemed to crawl. This was one of those times.

Kayleigh announced, "Boot-up complete. Self-diag-nostic in progress." Diana sighed and resisted the urge to pace. "Systems are good to go. When I hit the switch, the possibility of detection will kick up. We should hold until we're ready."

Diana turned to find Cara standing right behind her. At this moment, it was the other woman's responsibility to get the team prepared. Cara advised, "We're good to move."

Diana ordered, "Do it."

Kayleigh hit a button with a flourish. "All you, Deke."

The infomancer replied, "I have the signal. Okay, bots are active." Diana stared at the screen over his shoulder, which showed grainy black and white images in eight windows.

She frowned. "I thought you said you only had a couple."

"I lied." The distraction in his tone was a warning not to continue the conversation. She muttered to Cara, standing behind her, "Set up the teams in position to portal. Make sure Rath doesn't try to bring Max."

Her second-in-command chuckled. "Affirmative, Boss."

Deacon said, "Found a good spot. Back corner, no overlap from other anti-magic emitters, only one handling the room."

Diana asked, "Any chance it's that way as bait for a trap?"

On his screen, the windows converged on a thick cylinder covered in electronic-looking things. "Possible. Doubtful. Once you get in there and start and give me a bridge into whatever systems the enemy has running in the base, I'll know more. The bots are in position. Ready to go?"

She nodded. "Do it." She watched as all the boxes became filled with the cord connecting the device to the power grid.

Deacon said, "Using a heavy-duty model was smart, to ensure we couldn't somehow overpower it, although I don't even know if that's a thing. Still, it makes sense on the face of it."

He turned his head to grin at her. "The power draw is considerable, which means it has to stay connected to a source of electricity. If something should happen to that feed, well, let's just say it won't be good for the defenders."

Six of the eight screens went to black, and he finished, "RIP, little buddies. They died cutting the cord. Your path is clear."

Diana watched as Cara, Ruby, and Idryll were the first through the portal into the base. Their Magic City contact had insisted on coming along, and of course, that meant her companion had joined as well. Cara had promised to keep an eye on them, but that didn't change her responsibility to take that initial step.

Everyone else paused for a second to see if something bad would happen. When nothing occurred, the rest flowed through. The teams wouldn't use comms until Kayleigh and Deacon compromised the base's systems, which meant each team had prepared with a specific goal and several conditions that would cause them to abandon the fight and portal away.

Each group was targeting a different destination. Cara was headed to the armory because finding nonlethal weapons outside the base would be a highly annoying task compared to taking the ones they already had. Hank and Anik had perhaps the most unexpected role. *At least, hopefully the enemy won't anticipate it.* They were going to the vimana's core, what their expert mechanic liked to call the "engine room."

Diana had decided that if *they* couldn't use the vimana as a base, they certainly weren't going to allow the enemy to do so. While magic fueled the place, it still had mechanical systems, or at least they *looked* mechanical, as Hank explained it. The details didn't concern her, only the fact that both he and Anik had agreed that explosives should mess them up pretty effectively.

She, Rath, and Bryant were on the way to the vault to take away as many artifacts as they could. She was fully aware the move would make her look worse in the eyes of those who already suspected her. Still, she feared the evil potential of the objects and didn't want them in a bunch of bureaucrats' hands.

Long-term, she'd find someone she trusted and turn them over. Short term, the safest location for them was with her and her team. That left Tony and Sloan to hit Kayleigh's lab and grab whatever they could. With their backup base out of the picture, materials and supplies would be an ongoing challenge.

The other teams flowed out of the landing room on their way to split up at the nearest intersections. When an anti-magic emitter was in a hallway, they smashed it. They weren't willing to clear the place door by door to get them all. They couldn't afford the time, and they didn't have the personnel.

One member of each team carried network enhancers to put down at intervals when they split up. The devices would give Deacon more bandwidth to use to break into the base's systems. Diana had detailed herself to mount the one in their landing room, so their group was last to leave.

Bryant clubbed the anti-magic emitter into submission, ensuring that even if someone restored power to it, the unit wouldn't function. Rath twirled his batons, seemingly eager for the fight ahead. The troll said, "Max would've loved this."

Diana sighed. "Shut it. Get a move on, short stuff. You're on point." He laughed and scampered out the door.

She traded an amused glance with Bryant, obvious even through the team's masks that covered everything except their eyes. Certainly, Rath would be a dead giveaway about who they were, but her concern was for Ruby and Idryll, who definitely didn't need to have a confirmed spot on their enemy's hit list. She ran for the exit, Fury in her grip, ready to get a little payback.

Cara paused to attach a network enhancer to the wall, then spun in alarm as Ruby yelled, "Contact." The Mist Elf was mostly indistinguishable from the rest, having thrown on a loose shirt and pants to cover her identifiable leather armor and a mask to hide her face and hair. The tiger-woman was her twin and unfortunately would need to keep her claws sheathed to avoid outing herself. Their slight wardrobe change didn't appear to hamper their fighting effectiveness at all, though.

Ruby dashed forward toward the left member of the guard patrol. The base's defenders were armed with rifles and wore basic body armor. It was clear they'd achieved surprise, to judge by the shocked expressions and the lack of heavier equipment. *If the bad guys had known we were coming, they would've brought bigger guns.*

Ruby launched herself at the one on the left, and Idryll did the same on the right. Neither of them held weapons at the moment, but neither needed them. Both wore stun knuckles similar to the team's gloves, and *snaps* and *cracks* punctuated a flurry of punches as the electrical devices discharged. In only seconds, both men were down. Cara gave a nod of approval. "Nicely done."

Idryll laughed. "This is good. I needed some exercise. Too much time sitting around doing boring stuff."

Ruby's scowl was evident in her tone. "Doing my *job* is not boring stuff."

Cara sensed an argument, probably one they had often used to amuse themselves coming on and interrupted to stop it. "Onward. Remember the plan."

They both nodded, but she distinctly heard Idryll imitating her statement in a goofy voice. "Remember the plan." The shapeshifter continued in a normal tone, "Plans are boring. Improvisation, that's where it's at."

Cara sighed. *Here I thought that with Rath on Diana's team, I wouldn't have to deal with this sort of goofiness.* With a grin, she jogged after the other two, who had spotted another pair of guards around a corner and were charging to engage.

Kevin Serrano bolted upright in his chair, where he'd fallen asleep after a long day's work, at the chiming of his watch. He scowled down at the unfamiliar alarm, then realized what it meant. *Intruders in the vimana. Those clever scumbags.* He ran for the armory, Tash taking her place at his side partway there. He said, "Surprises galore with these people."

"Let's go show them how much we like the unexpected.

Which is to say not much. Not much at all. Just so we're clear."

He laughed at his second in command, then sped up so she wouldn't have the pleasure of outracing him to their destination by too many seconds.

CHAPTER THIRTY-ONE

Tony growled, "This sucks."

Sloan laughed. "You're not wrong."

Tony primed the grenade and threw it, wondering what it would do. They hadn't had a chance to practice with the gear Ruby had given them, and while she'd described the effects, he still hadn't seen them in action. It landed, discharged, and smoke billowed out of it. The pair of defenders ahead of them weren't wearing gas masks, and although they tried to turn and run, they only made it about two steps before stumbling, then falling to the floor.

They waited for the gas to dissipate, the vimana's circulation system running as efficiently as ever, then rushed forward, took the guards' rifles, and hogtied the men with zip ties. Their glasses weren't providing the tactical advantage they normally did because they lacked a central communication network to tie into.

Plus, not all the agents carried the advanced sensor packs they ordinarily did. It left them with only the short-range information their gear could provide, which was enough to warn them of nearby enemies. The tech had spoiled him. He missed having an eagle-eye view of the situation.

Sloan poked him in the shoulder. "Hey, partner, quit daydreaming."

Tony nodded. "I don't suppose either of those rifles is nonlethal?"

The other man shook his head. "Nope. Standard issue."

"This sucks."

His partner laughed. "Three more hallways to the lab. Let's get a move on." They found only one more pair of enemies along the way, which Sloan dropped with another gas grenade.

Tony heaved a quiet sigh of relief as the entrance appeared ahead and his glasses identified no enemies within their target destination. They dashed in and hit the button to slam the door closed behind them. It fell from the ceiling with a satisfying *clang*.

Added to that sound was an unexpected *whir*, and Tony spun to see what his eyes had initially glanced past, categorizing it as an irrelevant metal garbage can. It was rising to reveal tracked wheels underneath and extending what looked like gun barrels and other nasty weapons out of its carapace. "I think we have a problem."

Diana ducked behind the corner, annoyed at how quickly their enemies had marshaled a substantial response. She grabbed a stun grenade and threw it blindly, then stuck her head out to check the results. A flood of bullets caused her to jerk back again immediately, and she let out a loud curse in place of the yelp of alarm that wanted to escape. "Well, apparently those don't work against the upgraded version of the defenders."

Bryant chuckled. "They're not robots, *Boss*." He put a little humor into the last word since her callsign didn't adequately express their relationship.

She growled, "I wouldn't be too sure of that."

Rath, who had stuck his head around the corner low, reported, "Not advancing. Just staying there."

Diana nodded. "Because the longer they slow us down, the more people they can bring to bear. It's good to know they seem as interested in capturing us as killing us, at least."

Bryant replied, "That's because they don't know you." He held up a palm as he had multiple times since they'd entered the facility, then frowned at it. "Magic still being blocked."

She shook her head. "Have to give them credit for being smart about defending the place, especially given how unlikely it was that we'd come back here."

Rath said, "Time to Hulk it up?"

Diana nodded. "Condition Green, buddy. Do your thing."

Rath grew to his maximum size quickly, and she collected the gear that fell free in her left hand. Fury still filled her right, but he wasn't nearly the asset he usually was. She was serious about not wanting to kill anyone, which made the sword essentially a heavy stick to use as a bludgeoning weapon. While she was fairly sure she was skilled enough to stab and slice without killing, the consequences of an error were too high. *This is why we need our nonlethal equipment. Cara better pull that off.*

The now-eight-foot troll charged around the corner with a loud growl, and she and Bryant ran behind him. His vest hung on him, giving him some minimal protection against bullets, but several rounds still struck him as he advanced on the guards. Fortunately, when he grew, his skin got tougher. They didn't penetrate far. *Armor-piercing would probably be more effective but finding that ammunition inside the base would be a real surprise.*

He gave them the cover they needed to close with their enemies and slammed into the foursome at the end of the hallway. They were already stumbling backward in an attempt to disengage. He fell on two, smashing them down to the floor. She and Bryant engaged the others.

She raised her forearm to block her opponent's effort to use his gun as a club, the armor plate there easily absorbing the impact. Her right fist punched up into his triceps. When the pain distracted him, she landed an uppercut to the underside of his exposed jaw with her left. He went up on his toes, then fell, her stun glove rendering him unconscious.

Bryant's opponent hit the deck a moment later, and they moved on. The next corner revealed another pair of opponents, these decidedly more alarming. Diana gripped Fury with both hands, angling it defensively in front of her as the exoskeleton-equipped troops stomped forward.

They held shock batons, heavy clubs with tines on the end. The sharp points could kill if applied to a sensitive location, but their main purpose was to pierce armor protection so the discharging electricity would have the best path into an opponent's body.

The figures moved calmly, smoothly, showing mastery of the equipment. Diana growled, "Well, this sucks. Rambo, take the woman on the left. I've got the one on the right. Class, grab the network enhancer and put it on the wall. Then poke your head into the room beside us and see if there's an anti-magic emitter inside to wreck. Everyone, try not to get killed."

Her boyfriend replied, "On it."

Rath observed, "Those look nasty."

Diana nodded. "Avoid getting hit. Maybe try to bend the armor on their legs. A problem with exoskeletons is that they don't compensate for damage as well as unencumbered people can."

"Got it. Told you this would be fun." He rushed forward, and Diana raced toward her opponent, shaking her head. Her foe closed to meet her, clearing the area for his partner to take on the troll. The club swung down at her, and she intercepted it with Fury, stopping its descent cold.

She slammed the hilt back into the edge of the armor that ran along her opponent's ribs, hoping to break some important connection, but her strike completely failed to penetrate. She muttered, "Not cool," as she ducked under a swing from the second stun baton, which she hadn't realized he'd been carrying. Diana called, "Watch out, dual wield."

Rath replied, "More fun."

I really think we need to have a conversation about how you define fun. The two weapons came in slower than they might have without the exoskeleton, which was one of the reasons her team hadn't put any serious effort into using them in the field. They relied on speed and agility more than power, and exoskeletons didn't generally enhance those traits.

Despite having the technological advantage, her foe quickly demonstrated he wasn't as skilled as she was. He overswung with his right-hand club, causing his body to twist a little too much. In the moment it took for him to re-establish his balance, Diana rushed into his blind spot and slammed the hilt of her sword down onto the place where two pieces of exoskeleton met at the side of his knee. This time, it did some damage, denting the fragile area.

She leapt in the air, whipping Fury around at the back of his head, at the last minute twisting the blade so it crashed into his helmet rather than his bare neck. Her goal wasn't to penetrate but to force him to try to use the damaged joint. He stumbled forward, and when he stomped that leg down to catch himself, the metal bent more, then buckled.

He tumbled over, and she moved to help Rath. The troll eliminated the need, landing a punch with a shock glove right in the nose of his opponent, whose face mask was no longer attached. That one fell, and Diana tapped hers with a glove to put him out, too. Bryant reappeared on the scene. "No emitter. Nice work."

She growled, "Onward. They're getting organized way too fast."

Ruby shouted, "I have magic," and Cara immediately summoned hers, throwing a blast of force at the pair of guards hiding at the end of the hallway. One stuck his head around at the perfect moment to take a glancing blow from her spell and stumbled out into the intersection. Ruby's burst of shadow magic slammed him backward into the closed door of the armory.

Idryll ran forward, going low around the corner after the other guard. Sounds of blows landing came from her destination, and the shapeshifter reappeared a moment later to toss a rifle down the hallway past her. "Big guns, small skills."

Cara stepped to the armory and put her hand on the part of the wall that would sense its presence and open the door. Not surprisingly, it failed to work. She said, "Let's try telekinesis." Ruby nodded, and Cara reached out with her magic, trying to lift the door. It wouldn't budge. "They probably threw the bolts. We need to figure out a different way to get in there."

Idryll replied, "Think fast," and charged back down the hallway, where enemies had appeared.

She and Ruby spun to the sides, taking up the guards' former defensive positions. Cara leaned around the corner to throw another attack, only to realize these had different gear than the others, that backpacks were part of the difference, and that her magic was no longer reachable. With a growl, she ran down the hallway to assist Idryll.

The shapeshifter reached their foes before she did, knocking both rifle barrels up so their bullets hit the ceiling. The shapeshifter let out a low yelp, and Cara saw blood blossom along her side. She shouted, "You okay?"

Idryll slammed an elbow into the helmet of the one nearest her, then leapt to deliver a back kick that knocked the man backward. "Fine," she growled. "Flesh wound."

Cara laughed. "Just a flesh wound."

Idryll replied in an amused tone, "Exactly."

Cara's stun glove *snapped* as she punched her foe in the chin, but not as loudly as she would've liked. When she hit him again, it didn't go off at all. "Shit. Out of power."

Ruby slipped past her and delivered a front kick to her opponent, sending him to the floor with a clatter. The Mist Elf said, "Unless you have a great idea on the door, we're not in a very good position. Let's get rid of these back-packs, anyway."

Hank and Anik had made steady, stealthy progress toward the room located in the basement of the vimana. They'd chosen the sneaky path rather than the main door, a route through a small tunnel filled with conduits and thick cables that required them to crawl. Only the combination of their glowing watches and their glasses' low-light vision function allowed them to see anything at all. Finally, they dropped into the dimly illuminated space.

The room was full of things that looked like pipes and magical machines, things neither Hank nor Anik had the faintest understanding of. He'd spent most of a day in the space during their first week in the base trying to figure it out, then given up and ignored its existence after that. When he'd described it to their demolitions expert, Anik had been confident he could figure out how to mess it up.

It wasn't a guarantee that every important system went through that room. They couldn't guarantee that a complete set of redundant backups wasn't sitting ready to take over. There was no guarantee that their explosives could damage whatever the vimana's substance was. Still, they'd all agreed it was worth trying to deny use of the base to their enemies.

He crept to the exterior door, and his glasses informed him several heat signatures shaped like guards stood on the opposite side. He turned and whispered, "Stay quiet. Do your thing. If this door opens, hide."

Khan didn't reply. He kept planting explosives. When Kayleigh's voice suddenly sounded in his ear, it was a total shock. She said, "Comms are up, people. Deke is working on getting into the security system. Tell me what you need."

CHAPTER THIRTY-TWO

Cara looked back at the very-well-secured armory door with a growl of frustration. Kayleigh had reactivated the comms, which was a definite step in the right direction. *Here's hoping they can help us take another one.* She said, "Got any ideas on how to get whoever's locked in the armory out of there?"

The tech replied, "Wait one."

A few seconds later, Deacon joined the conversation. "The base's air circulation system doesn't have as much security as the rest of the stuff I'm trying to get into, so I have access. I think I can make it seriously cold in there."

"Will that damage the gear?"

"I should be able to find a temperature where they're really uncomfortable, but the equipment is unaffected. I'll do my best."

Cara said, "Well, if we can't open it, I guess it would be better if the gear doesn't work anymore. Do your thing."

She and Ruby took positions off to the sides, where no

one inside could shoot at them if the door suddenly opened. Idryll had moved down the corridor and stepped out of the hallway at the intersection, ready to alert them to enemy reinforcements coming their way. Deacon said, "Here we go."

It took almost a minute for anything to happen, a testament to the resilience of those inside. The infomancer provided a play-by-play of the temperature going down, but unfortunately, their lack of camera access meant they couldn't see the results. The loud metallic scraping of their opponents throwing the bolts gave ample warning, and when the enemy stumbled out, lifting weapons in limbs trembling from the cold, it was simple to disarm and subdue them.

Deacon quickly brought the temperature in the room back to something like normal, and she, Ruby, and Idryll slipped inside. Cara said, "Close the door and throw a couple of the bolts until we can get some surveillance." She switched to the comm channel that included everyone and announced, "Jewel, Cat, and Croft have taken the armory. Let us know if you're coming to join us."

The next thing she did, with great satisfaction, was to take the heaviest weapon in the room and use it to smash the anti-magic emitter into extreme dysfunction—which was to say, break it into pieces. She nodded in approval of her efforts. "All right, ladies. Bags are in the cabinet over there. Start filling them up. Nonlethal and defensive gear first."

Tony had both his pistols out and instantly moved to his right as the robot defender came to life. He squeezed the triggers quickly but calmly, sending anti-magic rounds to smash into the thing's skin. He growled, "Damn waste of expensive ammo. Doesn't seem to be doing anything."

Sloan had run and dived behind one of the lab tables, pulling it over as a shield in front of him. He shouted, "Grenade."

Tony scrambled away from the bot, then stumbled and fell as a burning sensation ascended from his calf to the rear of his thigh. His hands instinctively went to the pain areas and came back bloody. "I'm hit." He threw himself behind the nearest table and copied Sloan's move, knocking it over. He wasn't sure how long the metal would resist the robot's assault but figured anything was better than nothing.

The electrical grenade sizzled and spat, but the barrage from the mechanical menace didn't stop. Sloan yelled, "Flash-bang." It landed with a clatter and went off to a similarly negligible effect.

Should've brought heavier weapons. But no, we're trying to be nonlethal. The last word came out with a sneer in Tony's mind. He understood the need but didn't like the rule right at the moment. Out loud, he called, "Check the shelves."

Tony twisted toward the ones nearest him and started dragging down the unmarked black boxes Kayleigh used to store her creations. He removed the top of the first and found a series of canisters labeled "stun." They were bigger than the ones Ruby had provided, and he pulled the pin on one and tossed it.

In the interim, Sloan called back, "Nothing here. Going to try a web grenade."

Both munitions went off in quick sequence, the electricity seeming to cause the robot to pause for an instant before resuming its profligate shooting. *Or maybe it was reloading.* Tony peeked over the top to see that the web grenade had indeed locked their enemy in place, but motion wasn't essential to the thing's lethality.

Suddenly the guns fell silent, and the robot rotated to bring its other side to bear. A grenade sailed over his head and into the space behind them. Tony threw himself over his defensive barrier, spotting Sloan doing the same a moment after. The grenade detonated, discharging fragments of metal in all directions. His partner shouted in pain, but Tony had laid flat on the floor, and the ones that penetrated the table passed above him.

He snarled, "Screw it," and pushed himself up into a limping run toward the robot. It shot another grenade at him, but he slapped it away, his quick-draw skills giving him heightened reflexes in anything involving his hands. Sloan yelped and repositioned, but the grenade did him no damage when it went off.

Tony crashed into the robot, falling to lie on the floor beside it as it toppled. A blade shot out of it, and he wrenched himself back to avoid it. It pierced his vest, missing the plates and sinking into his stomach.

Fortunately, he thought he'd gained sufficient distance that nothing vital was damaged. He was out of ideas, but fortunately, he hadn't come alone. Sloan pushed a heavy 3D printer from a nearby shelf over onto the robot, and it smashed into its armor, broke off the blade that had plunged into Tony, and dented the metal enough that a piece of it lifted. The other man shoved an electrical grenade in there, then pulled him away before it went off. The spy collapsed on the floor beside him, panting. "Well, that sucked a lot."

Tony nodded. "I think I'm immobile for the moment. Hand me the heavy-duty med kit from that shelf, then smash the anti-magic emitter. We'll grab what we can and get the hell out of here. Oh, I almost forgot. Lock the door."

Sloan laughed and painfully climbed to his feet, wincing with each shift of position. "Good idea."

"Face?"

"Yeah?"

Tony let his head fall back on the floor, hoping the kit still held the local painkillers that should be in it. "Don't open the door to the computer area. If there's another robot in there, I'd rather not know about it."

Hank watched as Anik finished wiring up the various systems in the room. He wished he could see what waited on the opposite side of the door, but the techs hadn't gotten that far into the base's systems yet. *That's a point for the other team. If they have folks who are good enough to keep Deacon out of a system he's familiar with, they're a cut above most of the people we faced.* He called, "Almost done?"

Anik replied, "Settle down. You can't rush genius."

"You blow stuff up. That doesn't take genius."

The other man walked forward with a notably empty backpack slung over his shoulder. "What I do is an art. I don't simply 'blow stuff up.' I am the duke of destruction. The maestro of mayhem. The baron of bang. The —

Hank interrupted. "Babbling idiot."

Anik laughed. "So, timer's ready to go. We definitely don't want to be in here when the excitement happens, though."

"I hear that. Deke, any timeline on the cameras?"

The infomancer replied, "None. The base is fighting me. They installed their own AI. Bastards."

Hank rolled his neck. "Okay. The hard way, then." He lifted his stun batons, which were Rath's backup pair, fully charged and good for a couple of shots. Anik held an electrical grenade in one hand and the switch for the timer in the other. Hank grabbed one of the bolts securing the door and said, "We slide the latches, you start the timer, we rush outside, you pull the door closed behind us."

Anik nodded. "Do you want the option to stop the timer?"

Ordinarily, Hank would've said yes, but under-geared and unaware of what might await them outside the room, he shook his head instead. "No. We want this to happen regardless of whether we can handle whatever's out there."

His partner clipped the device on his belt and grabbed one of the slides with that hand. "Ready."

"Go." They yanked the bolts, opened the door, and charged out into the hallway. A team of four enemies waited, two a few feet away from the door down on one knee, the others several feet back. All of them had raised rifles pointing at the doorway. Hank went low as the gunfire began, sliding on the floor and whipping both batons around, crunching his core together for power in the awkward position.

The flexible metal poles slammed into the nearer pair, knocking them down despite their kneeling position. A grenade flew over his head and detonated with a sizzle, causing the gunfire from the back to fall off. Hank thrust himself to his feet and jumped over the nearer pair, counting on Anik to finish them. He rushed forward and whipped both batons inward, smashing them into the enemies' helmets, which then banged into each other.

The pair ended up dazed, whether from the impact or the grenade, and Hank delivered a series of punches to each that dropped them to the floor, their rifles falling away as they tried to protect themselves. He was adept at striking any part of the body, and it was a simple matter to avoid their body armor and make sure his knuckles met flesh. Eventually, the aggregate pain rendered them mostly immobile. He stopped punching and knelt to tie them up.

Anik laughed. "Feel better, Hercules?"

He joined in the mirth. "Actually, yeah. Do yours need a few reminders of why it's bad to mess with us, too?"

"Nah. Between the electricity I gave them and the damaged legs you provided, they've had plenty. I'll have them tied up in a second."

Hank toggled his comm to the group channel. "Twenty seconds or so until the base won't be quite as operational, maybe."

He turned to see Anik shaking his head. His partner

observed, "That's what I love about our jobs lately. The deep sense of certainty about everything."

He nodded. "Same here, my friend. We'll guard the door until they go off, then see what other trouble we can cause."

CHAPTER THIRTY-THREE

Kayleigh announced, "Red dots appearing. The anti-magic emitters must be down unless they've found a way to make the local penguins into combatants."

Diana suppressed a curse and continued to dash toward the vault. The door was closed, and she didn't have time to deal with unlocking it. She said, "Class, help me blast it." Every time she spoke his callsign, even now when things were tense, it made her think of their early days together, when he was Bryant Classified, to her.

He replied, "On three," and counted down.

At the appointed moment, she hit it with force magic as he did the same. The pressure wouldn't have been enough to get through the bolts if someone had thrown them, but it was sufficient to snap the latch that ordinarily kept it enclosed. The door swung inward, and they ran into the large room.

As they arrived, a portal opened, and two figures charged through it, followed by a third. Standard operating procedure was for the spellcasters to handle the magicals and Rath to deal with anyone who wasn't hurling magic. Diana dashed at the wizard, who was already waving his wand to send out an offensive spell. Bryant crossed behind her, going for the female magical whose ostentatious wooden bracelets were doubtless her wands. The troll ran up the middle toward the man in body armor.

Kayleigh said, "Did I mention there are a *lot* of red dots?"

Diana summoned a force shield onto her left arm and used it to intercept the thin line of flame emerging from the wizard's wand. She launched a burst of force at his feet, hoping to catch him off guard, but he nimbly skipped aside. She growled, "All right, people. Time to portal out."

Deacon interrupted, almost shouting, "I have cameras." Her glasses filled with their standard display, showing red dots and feeds from the cameras near her. She corrected, "Okay, keep at what you're doing, but as soon as there's a threat, get out. Do not let them capture you. Remember what I said."

She readied a fireball to throw at his face, then remembered the whole nonlethal thing. With a growl, she grabbed and tossed one of Ruby's electrical grenades at him, but he bounced it back at her with a look of condescension. She redirected it across the room, then focused on defending herself as the wizard summoned a wall of shadow and threw it at her.

Rath ran at the man, dodging and weaving to avoid bursts from his rifle. His batons were in his hands, and he used one to bat the weapon aside as he arrived. His opponent released it, and his right hand dipped down to his pistol while his left snapped out in the troll's face.

Impressive, not fazed by hitting a troll or by the fact that I'm smaller than him. We hate competent enemies. He'd heard other team members use the phrase often enough that it was now part of his regular vocabulary as well.

Rath bobbed his head out of the way of the punch and slashed his other baton at the man's feet. His foe brought his foot up in a quick kick to deflect the attack. Rath rushed forward, getting inside the man's angle with the pistol. He increased his size, reaching five feet by the time he stood toe-to-toe with the man and continuing to grow.

He'd assumed his opponent would be taken aback by the sudden change, but instead, he stepped backward, trying to bring the pistol around again. Rath slapped the gun from his hand with a quick baton strike and stabbed the other one at him. His enemy brought his arm up in a circle block to knock the weapon aside, avoiding the stun tip and kicked at Rath.

The blow hurt, knocked him back a step, a decidedly unexpected development. *He's got skills.* Another of the man's talents manifested as he yanked two long knives from behind his back and held them in the grip of an experienced fighter, the left one forward with point extended, the right one reversed along his forearm, ready to slice and stab with equal speed.

The troll smiled. "Fun."

Bryant spotted the witch's bracelets instantly and recognized them for what they were. When Diana angled at the male magical, he'd redirected toward the woman. Her face was neutral, and he imagined if they were in an action movie, she would say something like, "It's business, not personal."

It's pretty personal to me, gotta be honest. He summoned fire bolts with both hands, sending ten darts flying, each taking a different path, curving and twisting as they flew in at her. A small part of his mind had expected her to be impressed, or at least a little alarmed, but she simply waved, summoning a sheet of water in the air that hung there only long enough to extinguish his attack. She thrust her other arm forward, and a web of shadow flew out, growing as it moved.

The spell was unexpected, but he'd had lots of experience with adapting to unpredictable moments. He created an extra-long force sword in his right hand and slashed through the expanding net. With his other, he coated the floor under her feet with ice. Some of it latched onto her boots to hold her in place.

She shook her head. "Is this amateur hour?" A wave vanished the ice, and she skipped forward and punched with the other one, fast enough that the move had to be aided by magic.

The blow split his lip, and the taste of blood focused him. "Speak for yourself, lady." He created whips of force with each hand, sending one out to wrap around her neck and the other one down to entangle her feet. He yanked one hand to the left and the other to the right.

She managed to deal with the lower line but was pulled

off balance by the other. He summoned a portal behind her, then ran forward and jumped, kicking out with both feet.

The witch blasted him with force magic halfway there, taking away most of his velocity. Still, he outweighed her by a good bit, and mass mattered. His heels slammed into her chest, propelling her backward through the opening he'd created. He landed on his back hard enough to drive the breath out of him but closed the portal. *Ha. Wench. Now who's the amateur?*

Rath focused on blocking the incoming knife strikes, which were a blur of slashes and stabs. His skill with knives was more in the throwing of them, and he momentarily wished he'd chosen that option rather than moving close to engage. He'd been annoyed and had wanted the feel of direct contact. *Stupid troll is stupid. Well, maybe not stupid, but definitely indulgent.*

One of the strikes got through, scraping the skin along his forearm. The flesh underneath parted as well, and Rath pulled the injured limb back with a snarl. He tried to backpedal and disengage, dropping his baton and reaching for one of his throwing knives, but the man stayed with him. He grabbed the blade and launched it at his foe's feet, a weak throw meant mainly as a distraction. His enemy stopped and spun, narrowly avoiding having a knife sticking out of his foot. It gave Rath time to grab another, and he threw that one center mass.

The man whipped a knife across and blocked it, his

speed and control impressive. He dropped one knife and grabbed the rifle dangling from the strap one-handed, bringing it back up toward Rath. The troll growled, "No way," and snatched a grenade from his belt. He delayed several beats after priming it, counting the seconds off in his mind, then threw it at his opponent's face as he pulled the trigger.

Bullets flew over his head as he shrank to three-foot size and fell to his back. He watched the grenade smash into the man's head and go off, the *boom* of the concussion and bright light of the flash overcoming whatever defenses he might've had ready. His foe dropped his weapons, hands instinctively going up to cover his face. Rath leaned backward on his shoulders and flipped himself to his feet, eager to take his unexpectedly skilled opponent completely out of the fight.

Diana traded magic with the wizard, who, she had to admit, was rather talented. *Of course, if I was able to try to kill him like he's doing with me, things might be different.* That requirement had put her on the defensive, and she spent most of her time blocking his attacks and looking for an opening. When one came, she slashed a line of lightning along his leg, causing him to cry out in pain and start to limp. *Now I've got you, jerk.*

They both flinched when a concussion grenade went off beside them. Because it was one of Ruby's devices, her glasses and comm didn't get a signal to dampen the effect. He recovered a second faster than she did, and her last sight of him was as he opened a portal and dragged Rath's opponent through it.

She took a step toward the rift to follow, but a set of advancing figures in heavy armor carrying rifles filled the other side of the portal. She threw up a wall of force to keep them at bay and gave another order she didn't want to give, like the last time she'd been in the vimana. "Okay, people. Everybody out of the pool, right now."

Bryant created a portal, and they all dashed through it, headed to a neutral location in case anyone somehow followed. *Not a total win, but if all we accomplished was to put these scumbags on notice that we're not going to take their actions lying down, it was more than worth it.*

CHAPTER THIRTY-FOUR

The sense of togetherness was almost overwhelming after what they'd been through since being forced out of the vimana. Diana laughed inwardly. *We weren't even apart for that long. Is this what codependence looks like?* Ruby had brought several cases of beer from the nearby abbey, where the head Abbott was also a brewmaster.

The other woman had included four different varieties, and so far, Diana had thoroughly enjoyed the two she'd tried. The place didn't have a refrigerator big enough to handle that quantity, but when you had a bunch of magicals who could summon ice at will, such things weren't a problem. They'd repurposed one of the equipment cases as a cooler and were using several others as low tables to hold drinks and the many, many pizzas their host had provided.

Those rested in random places around the room, nothing in it capable of serving as a buffet, and Ruby unwilling to let her workshop be part of their revels. Rath and Max had dashed from one to the next, making sure to try each of them. The predictable argument about whether

261

pineapple belonged on pizza was happening in a corner, with the troll taking the position that *everything* was good on pizza and Sloan doing a series of imitations of famous people arguing against that opinion. They had attracted a small audience, and both seemed to revel in the attention.

Idryll and Ruby were deep in conversation with Tony, probably over something to do with law and order in Magic City. The young woman had taken a lot on her shoulders, both on this planet and Oriceran. Diana wished her well in those obligations. *I guess, while we're in this rebuilding phase, we'll have time to help her with some things if she needs it.*

Ruby's sister, Morrigan, had also joined them and was talking with Kayleigh. The gestures they shared suggested the potential for new tech arrows for the archer.

All in all, it spoke of family and safety. Something that had been clenched inside her stomach for days finally released. She looked over at Cara, who nodded and said, "Yeah. This is perfect."

Diana grinned. "Reading my mind, as always. I'm not quite sure of the next step. Hopefully, Deacon got some data we can use."

Her second in command shrugged. "All we need to do is stay safe and not arrested. After that, it's gravy."

Diana chuckled. "You know as well as I do that if we don't keep these maniacs occupied, they'll make us both crazy."

"True that." They shared a laugh, and Ruby walked over to stand nearby.

The *Mirra* of the mist elves asked, "What will you do now?"

Diana replied, "We found an ordinary everyday citizen up in Massachusetts infected with an artifact."

Ruby glanced down at her arm. "That's no fun." She knew firsthand since she was also an unwilling host to one of the magical items.

"Exactly. I wonder if it's more common than we think. If so, trying to find and help those people gives us an objective while we work on our big picture."

Cara added, "Plus, we need to scope out a new base. No offense, but this place is a little cramped."

Ruby laughed. "I get that. You all host the next pizza party. I'll expect local beer, though."

Diana nodded. "Done. Most importantly, we're going to figure out how to clear our names and get these bastards off our backs. It seems that this situation escalated unnaturally quickly. That tells me there's something more going on than is visible yet. Once I find out what it is, the real fun will begin."

Cara laughed and imitated Rath. "I'm so *very* in."

At the same moment, in an office park in Washington, D.C., Kevin Serrano sighed and leaned back in his chair, his eyes on the ceiling. "Those people suck. I still see stars."

Tash, across the desk from him, replied, "Seems to me that if that jerk was going to portal me somewhere, it could have been to the beach, rather than into a damn snowbank."

He laughed. "Could've been worse, I suppose."

She nodded. "A *lot* worse. He might have sent me to the World In Between."

Kevin knew enough about that dimension not to want anything to do with it. "You have to admit. It was a bold move on their part. Plus, they executed it well." He let his chair tilt forward and faced her.

She shook her head and crossed her arms. "I don't need to admit a damn thing."

"Don't be a bad sport. We're still in the early phase of a long match. When all is said and done, we'll wind up on top."

The witch grumbled, "Next time, I'm throwing that guy into a volcano. See how *he* likes extreme temperatures."

Kevin snorted. "Okay, Tash, let it go."

She sighed and made a visible effort to do so. "What's our next move? Vacation someplace warm and islandy?"

"Afraid not. I think we're going to have to turn to our NSA friends for a little help."

"Surveillance?"

He nodded. "*Total* surveillance."

"I read about something like that once. Wasn't that program shut down, considered too large an invasion of privacy?"

He shook his head. "You, of all people, should know by now that nothing useful is ever 'shut down.' It only gets renamed and buried deeper. A few days from now, assuming my connections are still intact, we'll have access to every camera in the country: military, police, civilian, whatever. If it communicates wirelessly or uses the Internet, we'll own it."

Tash nodded once, a look of satisfaction spreading

across her face. "They won't have anywhere to hide. I'll make sure the team is ready to deploy at a moment's notice."

"You do that." He picked up the phone. "Time for me to refresh some contacts and see what it'll take to get them dancing to our tune."

The story continues with book 2, *Rogue Agents on the Run,* coming soon to Amazon and Kindle Unlimited.

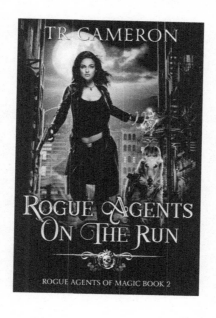

Thank you for reading the first book in this new series, and for continuing on to read these author notes! I am so very thankful for your interest in these stories and in whatever babble I put at the end.

Way back when (okay, a couple of years ago) when I finished the Federal Agents of Magic series, I didn't think I had more to say about them. In retrospect, I think I was probably just tired from life stuff and needed something lighter, which is why I shifted to the very fun Scions of Magic series with Cali and Fyre. Creating New Atlantis gave me a different creative outlet than working in the "real world" had. Magic City Chronicles did the same.

But what was strange was how the characters I thought I was done with kept showing up. Nylotte, Diana, Rath, and some of the others found their way into those other series. It made me realize for sure that I wasn't tired of the characters at all. Which led to the series you're now reading!

My amazing collaborators Martha Carr and Michael

Anderle are really good at laying out a path for their stories and following it, as near as I can tell. I'm... not. I start with a strong outline for a story, but it never, ever, EVER, winds up where I think it was going to. Which, to be perfectly honest, is a lot of the fun of the process for me. So, I'm very curious to see where this one goes. It's already taken a left turn from my initial plan, which didn't involve the counterattack on the Vimana. But that just seemed like the right thing for them to do, and after writing it, I think it was.

I expect Amadeo the assassin to return at some point. He was a fun character, and as I recall, Rath still owes him a favor.

I'm hopefully headed to Vegas for the 20Books show in November and will be around for the author signing event on Friday if everything works out. If you're going to be around, let me know, I'd love to say hi!

August is always weird for me. Like a lot of parents, my mental calendar more or less mirrors the academic year, so a new cycle is about to start. It gives me both stress and hope, that feeling of "Here's a clean slate, try not to screw it up this time." (My mind likes to suggest I'm not all that great at anything on a fairly regular basis. I ignore it, mostly. It's a thing we have.) So, here's to not screwing it up!

In the world of media content, I recently watched the 2009 *Friday the 13th*. Worst. Dialogue. Ever. But the opening sequence is a great piece of plotting. Also took in the first two *Fear Street* films, which I liked. Looking forward to *Free Guy* and *Shang-chi*.

I also watched *The Suicide Squad*, which deserves a special mention. Unlike most movies I like, which I can re-watch over and over, that one goes in the "Once is Enough" box. I really enjoyed it. The visuals were stunning, especially the look through Harley's eyes. Margot Robbie, Idris Elba, Daniela Melchior, and John Cena were all fantastic. But it was slow in parts, and kind of annoying in others, so i don't think I'll be back again.

Totally enjoyed *Loki*. I had my doubts, but they are definitely set aside. Haven't caught up with *What If* yet, but looking forward to it. The overarching story that the MCU has woven through its various properties is really impressive.

Humankind comes out this week. It's supposed to be the next best thing to *Civilization VI*, which I'm ludicrously addicted to. I'm hoping that it will be as fun as that game, which I could really use a distraction from. I've also agreed to join my kid for the next season of *Fortnite*, so if you're a gamer who plays that one, email me and let me know!

Reminder again - If you're not part of the Oriceran Fans Facebook group, join! There's a pizza giveaway every month, and Martha and (usually) I and all sort of fun author folks show up via Zoom to chat with our readers. It's a great time, and the community feel to it is truly fantastic. Oriceran Fans. Facebook. Your phone is probably within reach. Do it!

Before I go, once again, if this series is your first taste of my Urban Fantasy, look for "Magic Ops." I promise you'll enjoy it, and you'll get more of Diana, Rath, and company. You might also enjoy my science fiction work. All my writing is filled with action, snark, and villains who think they're heroes. Drop by www.trcameron.com and take a look!

Until next time, Joys upon joys to you and yours – so may it be.

PS: If you'd like to chat with me, here's the place. I check in daily or more: https://www.facebook.com/ AuthorTRCameron. Often I put up interesting and/or silly content there, as well. For more info on my books, and to join my reader's group, please visit www.trcameron.com.

AUTHOR NOTES - MARTHA CARR
SEPTEMBER 1, 2021

Lately, (and by lately, I mean the past eighteen months), I've been in need of a deep breath. You know the kind. It's not just any deeply inhaled breath. I do that at yoga a couple of times a week and every time my phone dings and reminds me. That last one is equal parts annoying and a good idea.

The kind of deep, fill-your-lungs and expand-your-chest breath I'm talking about is special. My brain disengages from past or present or a long to-do list and just – stops. Worry stops, weight lifts from my shoulders, and I suddenly can once again feel how I fit into things at large.

Fortunately, I'm a small and welcomed cog in a vast and complicated universe. I'm not supposed to be doing the heavy lifting of 'how do I get over there and make that particular thing happen'. Really, I'm supposed to be showing up and doing my part – and just my part – and having some fun while I'm at it.

I forget all of this from time to time and after the events of the past year and a half (you know the ones I mean), it's gotten even tougher. Lump on top of that cancer, chemo, redoing a garden during an unusually rainy season, and then recently, my sweet pittie Leela dying and, well, I had stopped taking those deep breaths. Certain things helped like a long swim or yoga, or just sitting on the back deck and listening to the water fountain. But it was temporary, and it didn't take much for me to slide back into a mild worry running behind everything.

That's no way to live.

So, last week I took off for Big Sur and stayed on an hundred acre property on a cliff above the ocean that was covered in an old redwood forest. Trails crisscrossed everywhere through the trees and ended at a large garden full of tomatoes and strawberries, mint and fig and peach trees and echinacea flowers and tall sunflowers. And chickens, of course.

My 'room' was a cabin on stilts with a view of the ocean way down below. Food was nearby as well as a hot tub with an infinity edge overlooking said ocean where I retreated every evening to look at a sky filled with stars. There was no light pollution so I could see more stars than I'd seen since I was a teenager camping in the Blue Ridge mountains of Virginia.

There was also no sound pollution, and I spent every morning making my way to the middle of the forest and then standing still – so I could hear nothing at all. That's when my brain finally let go and turned off. It was bliss.

It helped that for a few days a heavy fog descended among the trees only adding to the stillness. Things in the distance were either completely shrouded or barely outlined in the grey-blue mist. Thoughts about what to do next stretched only as far as my next destination, usually the garden, and I took in my surroundings without categorizing or questions. Instead, I was filled with wonder.

Space opened up and I felt myself taking in those deep breaths followed by nothing at all. I let go, at last of everything I can't control or fix or predict and was fully present. For me, that is the peace that passes all understanding – or explanation. It just is.

I'm grateful for the break and the reminder and my goal is to reach back to the memory of my week among the redwoods and pull that feeling back inside of myself. That way I can actually be present for those right around me, be kind in general, and actually have a little fun. More adventures to follow.

OTHER SERIES IN THE ORICERAN
UNIVERSE:

THE LEIRA CHRONICLES
CASE FILES OF AN URBAN WITCH
SOUL STONE MAGE
THE KACY CHRONICLES
MIDWEST MAGIC CHRONICLES
THE FAIRHAVEN CHRONICLES
I FEAR NO EVIL
THE DANIEL CODEX SERIES
SCHOOL OF NECESSARY MAGIC
SCHOOL OF NECESSARY MAGIC: RAINE CAMPBELL
ALISON BROWNSTONE
FEDERAL AGENTS OF MAGIC
SCIONS OF MAGIC
THE UNBELIEVABLE MR. BROWNSTONE
DWARF BOUNTY HUNTER
ACADEMY OF NECESSARY MAGIC
MAGIC CITY CHRONICLES

OTHER BOOKS BY JUDITH BERENS

OTHER BOOKS BY MARTHA CARR

JOIN THE ORICERAN UNIVERSE FAN GROUP ON FACEBOOK!

CONNECT WITH THE AUTHORS

TR Cameron Social

Website: www.trcameron.com

Facebook: https://www.facebook.com/AuthorTRCameron

Martha Carr Social

Website: http://www.marthacarr.com

Facebook: https://www.facebook.com/groups/MarthaCarrFans/

Michael Anderle Social

Website: http://lmbpn.com

Email List: http://lmbpn.com/email/

https://www.facebook.com/LMBPNPublishing

https://twitter.com/MichaelAnderle

https://www.instagram.com/lmbpn_publishing/

https://www.bookbub.com/authors/michael-anderle

Made in the USA
Las Vegas, NV
11 October 2023